Switchback

Frank LaCrosse watched the morgue attendant pull the two drawers from the wall. Inside each was a body.

The morgue attendant matched the tag numbers of the cadavers against those on the computer printout in his hand. Satisfied they were the right decedents, he stepped back to let the FBI agent inspect them.

Frank had already snapped on a pair of thin latex gloves and now went to work examining the two cadavers. He did so with a clinical detachment that went with his straight, regular features and the camel-wool topcoat worn over the dark suit, all of which J. Edgar Hoover would have readily approved.

"You ever seen anything like that before?" asked the morgue attendant as LaCrosse finished his examination and began removing his rubber gloves.

The FBI man regarded the morgue attendant dispassionately for a long second.

"Yes," he said.

SWITCHBACK

A novel by
DAVID ALEXANDER

Based on the film written and directed by
JEB STUART

AVON BOOKS ◆ NEW YORK

AVON BOOKS
A division of
The Hearst Corporation
1350 Avenue of the Americas
New York, New York 10019

™ & © 1997 Paramount Pictures. All Rights Reserved.
Based on the motion picture by Rysher Entertainment and Paramount Pictures
Visit our website at **http://www.AvonBooks.com**
Library of Congress Catalog Card Number: 96-96457
ISBN: 0-380-79022-X

First Avon Books Printing: November 1997

AVON TRADEMARK REG. U.S. PAT. OFF. AND IN OTHER COUNTRIES, MARCA REGISTRADA, HECHO EN U.S.A.

Printed in the U.S.A.

WCD 10 9 8 7 6 5 4 3

And thus I clothe my naked villainy,
With odd old ends stol'n forth of holy writ,
And seem a saint when I most play the devil.

—*King Richard III*, Act I, Scene I

1

The neo-Victorian house occupied a two-acre lot on a residential street in Alexandria, Virginia.

It was close to nine o'clock on the evening of a hazy summer day. The sun had set half an hour before. The porch light was turned on.

Inside the house, little Andy's baby-sitter, Missy, was giving him a bath. The one-year-old boy splashed around in the large acrylic tub, animatedly working his small arms and legs.

Missy, a woman in her forties, had her hands full keeping the boisterous tot from soaking the entire bathroom.

Enough was enough, she told herself, grabbing a fluffy pink towel from the rack behind her and laying it across the top of the nearby toilet.

"Come on now, Andy," she said to the misbehaving boy good-naturedly. "Time to dry off."

Lifting the toddler out of the soapy water, Missy wrapped him in the towel and carried him toward the bedroom adjacent to the bath.

"Your folks are gonna be home soon, darlin'," she cooed at the boy as she toweled his hair dry. "And they'll be mighty cross with me if you're still up."

As she dressed him in his pajamas, Andy twisted and turned playfully. "Now, hold still," Missy told him. "Gotta get you ready for bed."

She heard the sound of the bell from downstairs and stopped in midsentence.

Now who could that be? It was too early for her employers, and besides, they had the key.

The bell rang a second time. Missy quickly finished toweling Andy off and put him in his crib.

"Now you be good," she admonished him. "Play with your train and Missy'll be right back." The boy began to roll a small red locomotive engine over and around his blue blanket.

Missy went downstairs and looked through the peephole of the front door.

At first she saw nothing but an amorphous gray blob.

Then the man standing on the porch stepped back, and Missy got a good look at him.

Early thirties, sandy brown hair neatly cut,

wearing a dark business suit. He was carrying something, but she couldn't make out what it was. Maybe a briefcase, maybe a carryall; Missy couldn't tell which.

Missy felt an inexplicable fear of the stranger. If he were a salesman, why would he be coming by so late? If his car had broken down, where was the car? She didn't see one behind him.

"Yes?" she said tentatively, loud enough to be heard through the solid oak door.

"Evenin', ma'am," the man replied in a friendly voice with faint southern overtones. "Would Frank or Jean be at home?"

"No, I'm afraid they're not," Missy answered, her fear eased by his amiable manner and voice. "They'll be back shortly, though."

"You must be Missy," the man went on without hesitation. She saw him smile.

"Yes," she said after a beat, and her unease returned. How would he know her name? She supposed the parents could have told the visitor that.

"Forgive me for not introducing myself, Missy," the man went on in his smooth, friendly way. "I'm Tom Bellingham. I'm an old friend of Jean's from Denver. Told her last week I'd be stopping by to say hello."

He paused and flashed Missy another smile through the peephole. "When was it you said they'd be back again?" he asked.

Missy hesitated but chided herself for being so paranoid. Frank and Jean probably had told him to come over, just like he'd said.

She unlatched the door and opened it a crack, though she kept the security chain in place.

"They should be back in around thirty minutes."

The stranger glanced at his watch.

"Darn," he said. "I believe I'm gonna have to miss them. Y'see, my plane leaves in an hour." He flashed Missy his smile again.

"Missy, would you do me a big favor?" he now ventured. "Would you kindly tell Frank and Jean that I just dropped by to steal a peek at my little Andy? My wife would kill me if I came all the way from Denver without saying hello."

Missy found herself fingering the latch on the security chain but thought better of it. He sure was slick. But he could be anybody when you got right down to it.

"I'm sorry, Mr. Bellingham," she said firmly to the man on the porch. "They'll be home real soon."

The visitor's smile faded and his eyes took on a look of sadness. He glanced down for a moment.

"Sure," he said, sounding dejected. "I understand. Don't you worry 'bout it none."

Missy shut the door and turned the latch, locking it. Then she peered through the peephole.

The man still stood there, as though he were making up his mind to say something else. But a second later he turned and Missy watched him descend the brick stairs into the wide circle of porch light cast onto the front yard. He hesitated again, looked to his right, then took the walk left to the driveway, and then, quickly to the street. A moment later, he was swallowed up by the darkness.

Missy went back to the stairs. She'd climbed partway to the landing when she heard a sound coming from the back of the house.

She stopped and listened.

There was nothing.

Must have imagined it, she thought.

She began mounting the stairs when she heard it again. It was a faint tinkling sound. Like glass breaking.

Missy went down the stairs and into the kitchen. It was dark, and she flipped the switch near the entrance to turn on the overhead light.

Her eyes darted everywhere when the light came on, as though she expected to be shocked and wanted to get it over with as quickly as she could.

But the kitchen was empty.

Crossing to the back door, Missy checked the lock and found it bolted securely.

As the hammering in her chest abated, she flipped off the kitchen light and went back to the stairs. Now a dull thud came from above, and the hammering started again, double time. She took a step up, but as hard as she strained, heard nothing. Missy took another step, and a third, and just as she was about to hustle the rest of the way up, the family cat rushed around the corner and shot through her legs.

Missy grabbed the railing with one hand and slapped the other to her chest. Catching her breath, she turned and watched the cat disappear into the kitchen. It would be a long time, she thought, before she let *that* creature on her lap again.

Smiling at her folly, she reached for the light switch again to make sure the cat didn't get into any more mischief.

She didn't live to touch it.

Black-gloved fingers locked themselves around Missy's forearm as another hand was clamped over her mouth, and she was pulled from the doorway into the kitchen.

Missy struggled with all her might, but it did her no good. Her attacker was far too strong. She might have struggled harder had she seen the eight-inch knife blade gleaming as it slid between her legs, but she couldn't, and besides it wouldn't have helped any.

She didn't have a chance.

Her attacker knew that, and he took his time with the knife, sliding it up along the inner part of Missy's thigh. Her eyes went wide with terror as she felt the chill defilement of the cold metal against her flesh.

In another second, the tip of the blade touched the round of thigh just below Missy's crotch. It lingered there for an instant, and then she felt it thrust up hard. Waves of blinding pain strobed through her.

A second later Missy's world went dark forever.

The attacker saw her legs stop thrashing and felt her grip loosen on his arm.

Gone, he thought with satisfaction.

He laid the woman's corpse gently on the floor.

The killer deftly sidestepped the leading edge of the blood-spill, which ran along the linoleum, and walked toward the door, not getting so much as a drop on his boots. He'd done this before. And practice, after all, made perfect.

The killer slowly took the stairs to the bedrooms on the upper story of the house. He didn't rush.

The man had a sixth sense when it came to these things. He knew he didn't have to rush. As he climbed the stairs, a song came into his head. It was an old song, dating back to pioneer days.

Let me sing you a song 'bout sweet Betsy from Pike, he thought as he hummed the familiar tune, and then began singing it out loud in midverse, "Who crossed the wide mountains with her lover Ike . . ."

. . . With an old Shanghai rooster and an old yaller dog, the words went on in his mind as he reverted to humming, absently straightening a painting near the top of the landing with his tight-fitting black gloves.

Still humming, the killer entered Andy's room, leaving his back to the door. He watched the toddler play for a moment, then pulled a patchwork quilt off the bed—one his grandmother made just for him, using pieces of his father's baby clothes—and bent to wrap Andy in it.

Andy cooed at his new playmate and snuggled into the quilt.

"Come on, partner," the man said, lifting Andy from the crib.

Then the killer turned off the bedroom light and walked back down the stairs with the baby cradled in his arms.

2

Three months later

Winter in Amarillo, Texas, came early this year and was lingering far too late. It had already overstayed its welcome by at least a month.

Perhaps the winter would have been made more palatable by a gentle snowfall or even the hope of one. Perhaps a little rain would remind the winter it should be spring. But the rough gray sky, if it promised anything, promised only storms and bitter cold, while the wind rode hard across the Panhandle.

At a railroad crossing a late-model Ford rumbled in a shadow of a speeding train. It was emblazoned with a five-pointed star and the words "Amarillo Sheriff." Exhaust riffled around it and condensation clung to the edges of its windows.

Behind the wheel, Deputy Sheriff James McWethy looked straight ahead, carefully counting a long string of green boxcars slowly trundling past. He didn't want to risk saying anything to the man sitting beside him.

Sheriff Buck Olmstead was not in a talkative mood these days, Deputy McWethy knew, nor did McWethy especially care to let his eyes wander to either side.

On the right, sat the sheriff. On the left, rising above the roadside on thirty-foot-high metal legs, was a gigantic campaign poster emblazoned with the smiling face of city police chief Jack McGinnis, the man who was not only running against Olmstead in this year's election but who had a damn good chance of beating him to boot.

The young deputy was caught between the proverbial rock and a hard place, and knew it. He kept staring at the line of slow-rolling boxcars, wishing they'd move a little faster so he could get the hell out of there.

Five minutes later, they were still sitting in the motionless vehicle, and it was the sheriff who finally broke the silence.

Olmstead had a raspy voice, and the rest of him more or less went with his voice. At the age of fifty-five, he preferred street clothes with a western cut to a uniform. His was the demeanor and the dress of a man with nothing to prove because his legend spoke louder than any command or outfit. He was a twenty-five-year veteran of the Amarillo Sheriff's Department. He had a room full of citations for bravery. More importantly, he had hitmen's respect.

And Olmstead's actions had never been soft.

"My God, that man can smile," Olmstead remarked, not looking at the deputy.

McWethy didn't answer, and thanked the Lord that the sheriff really hadn't expected a reply.

The last car of the freight train passed them by. The deputy put the car into drive and rolled across the tracks.

Olmstead didn't say anything else as the campaign poster slid past. He imagined it watching him, though, and laughing.

The parking lot of the Tall Indian Motel was bookended by a Gulf station on one side and a junkyard on the other. Today the lot, which was normally occupied only by a few dust-caked pickups belonging to local cowboys, was wall-to-wall with well-scrubbed vehicles from the sheriff's department.

Amidst the many tan uniforms moving bus-ily around the lot, the driver of a parked county ambulance leaned against his hood, smoking a cigarette. His partner had gone around the corner for coffee and donuts. The coroner was inside, and the ambulance crew was just waiting around to be called up with the stretcher to remove the body from the premises.

The ambulance driver's eyes flicked to the car that had just entered the lot.

He recognized Olmstead as he got out of the shotgun seat. It meant things would start moving fast, from here on out.

Olmstead greeted the driver with a brief inclination of his head as he passed. They had seen each other enough times before to forego words at times like these.

The driver finished his cigarette and crisscrossed the glowing tip against the side of the ambulance. His partner was coming up the walk with a brown paper bag in his hand.

He glanced after Olmstead, then took a sip from the cup his partner had handed him. "I told you cream but no sugar in mine," he said, but decided not to throw it out. Instead he sealed the top again and wrapped his hands around the cup. When you live in the world of the dead and dying, any little warmth is savored.

Room 103 occupied a corner of the Tall Indian. Over the years it had witnessed its share of lovers' trysts, tired businessmen, drunks, and transients. But today was a first.

Today there were two corpses lying in the bathroom of 103.

Olmstead found the motel room thronged with Northwest Texas cops. He knew every one of the deputy sheriffs in the place, and they all knew Olmstead.

Silence instantly took command of the room. Every man's face turned to Olmstead, like sunflowers pointing into the light. Olmstead nodded to a young officer as he came in.

Bud Lomax beamed slightly, as if Olmstead had just laid a hand on his shoulder and shared some confidence or old lawman's secret, remembering, though, to show the reserve the situation dictated. Just as his father, one of Olmstead's partner's long ago, had taught him.

"How's your pa, Bud?"

"Better, Sheriff," the deputy answered, feeling flattered that Olmstead had taken notice of him. "I'll tell him you asked."

"You tell him to stay off that leg, hear?"

"Sure will, Sheriff."

Olmstead went past the deputy into the center of the room, where Sim Jackson, the county coroner, was making his way toward him.

Olmstead and Jackson went back awhile. Sim was a compact man with a long, bony face dominated by a pair of washed-out blue eyes. Olmstead always thought they'd gotten more washed-out over the years. As if each new corpse he examined took a little something away from Sim's immortal soul.

"Buck," he said by way of greeting.

"Sim," Olmstead replied in kind. "You want to tell me about it?"

"Ain't so bad," Sim said.

He gestured at Olmstead to follow him into the bathroom.

Cops were clustered around the bathroom door, blocking Olmstead's view of the interior as he approached. It took a moment for them to part so he could enter. The sight that greeted Olmstead's eyes made him wonder what the coroner *would* consider "bad."

"Never trust a coroner," he muttered, going into the bathroom.

The murder scene registered on Olmstead's experienced eyes in a series of discrete images.

Blood. It covered the walls and the floor. It ran in tracks down the edge of the toilet and spattered the plastic seashell-patterned shower curtains. It stained the bath towels and the mirror of the medicine cabinet that hung ajar over the bloodstained sink.

Corpses. The naked corpse of the male victim and the fully clothed corpse of the Korean housekeeper lay entwined in a garish embrace. Both cadavers were also covered with blood.

The woman lay across the man's body, her legs splayed above his face, her head on his groin. By the severe backward tilt of the woman's head Olmstead knew her neck had either been broken or her throat deeply cut.

Olmstead had seen enough. He slid off his

glasses and wiped them with a handkerchief he pulled from his jacket. It was a sign to his men that he was done looking; now it was time to question and think.

"Severed femoral artery in the groin area on the male decedent," Sim recited from his notes as Olmstead wiped the lenses of his glasses. The coroner's voice had taken on a familiar tone of clinical detachment. "Single, almost surgical cut," he went on. "Whoever done this knew what he was doing. Nothing tentative about it."

Jackson looked up at the blood-batiked walls of the cramped motel bathroom. "Must have been an artesian well in here for about thirty seconds."

"Girl too?" Olmstead asked, remembering the odd cant of her head, glad that the bodies were no more than expressionist blurs with his glasses off.

"No," Sim said, shaking his head. "Throat was cut, probably in the other room. Then she was brought in here." Sim closed his spiral pad and tucked it in his pocket. "I can give you more when we get them out of here."

Olmstead nodded at Jackson. Putting his glasses back on, he went back into 103's main room as the two ambulance attendants entered.

Olmstead nodded at them and they brushed past him on their way into the bathroom carrying a collapsible stretcher. Olmstead's glance fell on the motel room's two single beds. Both, he noticed, had been turned down and looked slept-in.

"How you holding up?" Sim asked, having walked up behind the sheriff. Olmstead knew what he was referring to. It wasn't the murders.

"Hell, when have you known me to worry about an election?" he replied, hoping Sim wouldn't notice the lie.

"Never. Then again, I've never known anyone with a chance of beating you before." Sim patted Olmstead on the back. "Hang in there, Buck," he said, and headed for the door.

Olmstead turned to the motel room's TV, which had been left on and tuned to a twenty-four-hour cable weather channel.

He watched the most recent forecast scroll across the bottom of the screen, his mind only half-registering the prediction of heavy snowfall ahead and travel advisories in the mountains. Still looking at the TV, he called for his chief deputy, Nate Booker.

"Sheriff?" Nate, a tall man in his late thirties asked.

"Your report," Olmstead told him. "Let's have it."

Nate flipped through a spiral pad and began.

"The man registered is Bill Suderland.

Home, Fort Worth. He checked in alone but paid for two. Also paid for the room with cash. The owner remembered he had a roll of bills thick enough to choke a horse. Haven't found it or a wallet yet. Had a car. That's missing too."

"What . . ."

Olmstead fell silent as he saw the first body carried out. It was the woman's. Olmstead didn't turn away. Out of respect. He wanted to show her if she was looking down at him that he wouldn't ignore or forget what happened here.

He noticed Bud had followed his lead. He'll be a good cop, he thought. I'll have to remember to tell his father that.

"What about the girl?" Olmstead continued after the stretcher went out the door.

"She was a maid here at the motel," Booker replied. "It's a family place. Best we can tell, she must've walked in on it."

Olmstead shook his head as the second body was now brought out.

"What else?"

"That's about it," Nate told him after a beat. "We've taken hair samples that seem to match Suderland's from one of the beds. The other was slept-in but clean."

Olmstead shot Nate a look that the deputy knew all too well.

"We'll check it again," he said sheepishly.

*   *   *

The ambulance crew had left the parking lot. Sim Jackson's car was long gone. For a moment the wind had abated as well, as if it had followed the dead.

Olmstead and Nate stepped into the Tall Indian's restaurant, where several of the waitresses sat at a booth in the back, consoling each other.

Behind the counter the owner had his arm around his wife, who dabbed at her eyes with a ball of crumpled white tissue.

Park Van Nam had come to America from his native Seoul to escape the tyranny of his homeland. He found plenty of the same in Texas, though.

Park had no illusions any longer. The law had failed him one time too many. He glared at Olmstead and Nate as they approached.

"Sheriff, this is Mr. Nam," Nate told Olmstead, making introductions. "He owns the place." He paused a beat and looked away from the smaller man's hate-filled eyes. "It was his daughter," he said in a changed voice.

"I'm very sorry, Mr. Nam," Olmstead told the bereaved man. "But I give you my word. We'll catch the killer."

Park looked at Olmstead without uttering a syllable for a long moment. When he finally spoke it was in a low, controlled voice that cut Olmstead like the edge of a razor.

"Just like you caught the men who rob me?" Olmstead turned to Nate.

"What robbery?" he asked the deputy.

"The restaurant's been robbed twice in the last six months, Sheriff," Nate replied, this time avoiding both Park's and Olmstead's eyes.

" 'Trust us.' That's what your deputies say each time they come," Nam put in, his voice rising with anger. " 'Don't worry.' 'Trust us,' he mimicked, singsong fashion. "*Now* see what happens!" He delivered his last sentence as a shout of rage.

Olmstead watched Nam take his sobbing wife in his arms and speak to her softly in Korean. He rocked the grief-stricken woman in his arms, cradling her like a child.

Olmstead felt a ball of heat rise from the pit of his stomach as he watched the owner and his wife. He turned away, looking up at the ceiling. His eyes narrowed to slits as he saw two security cameras above the cash register and exit.

"Those things working?" he said to Nate.

Figures moved in slow motion across the black-and-white screen of the motel's security system. Olmstead, Nate, and a deputy stood in the motel's office, watching a segment of the videotaped feed of the last twenty-four hours.

A tall, rangy looking man and a little girl in jeans and a checked western shirt moved toward the restaurant's door. They were accompanied by a casually dressed man in his twenties, who somehow didn't look like a local to Olmstead.

"He put them up after the second robbery," Olmstead heard Nate's voice tell him as he stood with his eyes riveted on the screen. "We're pulling the four hours surrounding the murders."

Olmstead continued watching the figures move toward the door at one-half speed.

"We don't know if he even came in here or who we're looking for. But at least it's something," Nate went on.

"Soon as you can, bring in the waitresses," Olmstead answered, continuing to watch the spectral figures vanish through the restaurant's entranceway. "See who they know. Regular customers first and work back from there."

Nate nodded and walked away. Olmstead rewound the tape and turned back toward the console.

The wind roared back as Olmstead and Nate came out of the Tall Indian's rear office and walked toward their vehicle.

Olmstead immediately noticed the city black-and-white angle-parked among the tan sheriff's department cars. The city police vehicle stood out like a penguin in a herd of antelope.

The sheriff's eyes flicked from the car to a well-dressed man in a gabardine suit who leaned against it with a casual ease, talking with some of Olmstead's deputies. Then the dude flashed a hundred-kilowatt smile at one of the cops. It was the same smile on the campaign poster Olmstead'd seen at the railroad crossing.

"Oh, Christ," Olmstead said softly. "McGinnis."

Suddenly McGinnis looked up and spotted Olmstead. He waved at the sheriff.

"Looks like a bad one, Buck," he called out. "Thought I'd come by and see if you needed any help."

"Mighty nice of you to offer, Jack," Olmstead returned in a saccharine voice. "Maybe your boys could handle the traffic control out on the street."

Olmstead's smile was a perfect match for the voice. It was tight and it was phony.

McGinnis's neon-bright smile went suddenly dark. That wasn't exactly the kind of help he'd had in mind.

"A lot of people are gonna be concerned about this one when they hear about it, Buck," he retorted, the mock-friendly attitude now entirely absent. "If this guy turns up in my jurisdiction, don't expect a courtesy call."

"If he shows up in your district, he's as safe as a church mouse," Buck replied.

McGinnis brusquely turned and climbed back into the black-and-white, his driver getting in on the opposite side.

Buck wondered if McGinnis had ordered his driver to take up two parking spots.

As the car pulled out, McGinnis rolled down the window and asked, "By the way, have you seen my billboards?" Then he rolled the window shut, smirking.

Olmstead continued to smile as the car executed a tight K-turn, and sped toward the entrance, tires squealing.

Even before it left the lot, Olmstead was no longer smiling. McGinnis had laid it all on the table.

In order to win the election, Olmstead knew he'd have to find the killer. If he didn't, McGinnis would be sheriff come election day. It was, as they said in those parts, country simple.

Olmstead turned to his deputy.

"What about the missing vehicle?" he asked Nate.

"Ford Explorer. Nineteen ninety-four. Red. Texas plates. Highway Patrol's got the word out on it."

Olmstead looked back at the motel, staring hard.

"Find it," was all he said.

3

The pickup rolled along the deserted two-lane back road beneath a sky the color of wet slate. The road dipped and swayed like a sidewinder as it followed the undulating contours of the desert landscape.

Inside the truck, Lane Dixon watched the little girl draw his picture with a set of crayons. Her rendering of Lane looked like a cubist vision of a T. Rex.

"Like it?" she asked.

"It looks just like me," Lane told her.

The girl smiled and went back to her drawing.

"Comin' up on our turnoff," the weather-beaten rancher said to Lane from behind the wheel of the pickup, indicating the dirt road up ahead. "Sure you won't come up and stay with us for the night?" The little girl looked up at Lane, expectation filling her big blue eyes.

"Thanks," Lane told the rancher. "But I

23

need to get a little farther up the road before dark.''

"Well, just don't get stuck out here if this storm hits,'' the driver told him as he slowed the truck at the dirt road and idled the engine.

Lane climbed out of the truck and lifted his pack up out of the cargo area behind the cab. Waving to the rancher's daughter, he began walking along the main road.

The rancher put the pickup in gear and drove off. His little girl gave him a long look, which he didn't return. She went back to her drawing.

A station wagon was coming up the road as Lane trudged along the shoulder. It was almost too good to believe.

Lane stretched out his right arm and raised his thumb, hoping to hitch a ride, but the car didn't stop. He looked down the empty road and wondered how long it would be till another car came by.

A long time, probably.

Lane had no choice but to start walking again. It was too cold to stand in one place with darkness coming on. He pulled up his coat collar against the razor-edged wind and continued walking up the road.

It was a lot darker by the time Lane reached the crest of the mile-long up-slope that the road now took. At the top of the rise, he looked down into endless miles of desolation, unbroken by even the flicker of light from the porch of a distant ranch.

With a sinking feeling in his gut, Lane realized he was alone in the middle of nowhere, with a long, dark night as his only companion.

Suddenly he heard the deep rumble of a truck behind him. Turning, he looked into the blinding glare of the headlights of the vehicle.

It was coming on fast, doing at least ninety per. Lane stepped back onto the shoulder and held out his thumb. The truck kept right on going.

It was gone in a blink.

Lane turned dejectedly, startled by the approach of a second vehicle that was riding in the wake of the big eighteen-wheeler. Trucksucking, they called it in those parts.

Lane tried to flag it down too, but the white Eldorado was already going past him as he extended his arm.

Lane turned and followed it with his eyes, hoping against hope that the driver would pull over and stop. But it was already a good hundred yards down the road.

Lane put his hand down. He'd missed his chance.

At that moment he saw the Caddy's two red wedge-shaped brake lights flare and the car come to a sudden halt.

Lane loped down the hill as the Caddy reversed toward him. When it stopped a foot or two ahead, Lane opened the big door and threw in his pack.

But when the driver pushed the forward-leaning passenger seat back so Lane could get in, Lane saw something that stopped him dead in his tracks.

The Caddy's interior was covered from dashboard to dome light with glossy pictures of naked women clipped from girlie magazines, pinup calendars, and French decks. Every available inch was covered with them—front seats, rear seats, dashboard, floor mats, even the steering wheel and column.

Everything except the windows. And every one of the photos was protected by some kind of clear plastic covering.

Lane stood there holding the open door, wondering if he should just grab his pack out of the rear and take his chances on the road instead of accepting a ride from an obvious head-case.

Lane's eyes flicked to the lean-jawed man sitting behind the wheel.

He was a cowboy type, wearing jeans and a denim work shirt with the sleeves rolled up to the biceps. There didn't look to be any flies on him, and there definitely weren't any beaver shots on him.

He grinned at Lane from under the brim of his cowboy hat.

"Well, get in, boy!" he said to the hitchhiker.

"I can't heat this damn car and the whole New Mexico desert too!"

Lane pushed aside his unease and edged his body into the Caddy, noticing even the door handles were covered with plastic-coated girlie pix.

The second Lane closed the door, the driver put the pedal to the metal and jackrabbited the Caddy down the road. All four door locks automatically snapped down into their sockets with a loud, simultaneous bang.

"Always drive this heap with the doors locked and the seat belts on," the driver explained, still grinning like a mule in clover. "Habit's what it is. You could say I'm a creature of habit."

Lane took his cue and pulled the seat belt out of the niche to his right. Like the driver's, it too was covered with pictures of naked women.

"Some collection, huh?" the driver said with pride as Lane buckled up.

"Yeah," Lane answered, not knowing what other comment he could make under the circumstances.

"You're not gay, are you?"

"No," Lane replied, "it's just that I've never seen anything like this."

As the car sped along the road, the driver flipped on the overhead dome light so Lane could get a better view of his bizarre job of automotive interior decoration.

"Y'all should have seen my first one," he told Lane. "Eighty-two Eldorado. Had my girls all lacquered on with a liquid sealer. Man, it sure was a beaut. But after awhile, you know, your tastes change. You get tired of looking at the same old faces and all."

The driver stole a look in the rearview at the road behind and goosed the accelerator up another ten miles per.

He went on, "So when I ran out of room to put up any new ones, well shoot, I had to sell her. Man, I had me a heck of a time gettin' rid of that old car."

"I bet," Lane answered.

"But now, this honey . . ."—the driver lovingly stroked his hand across the top of the dash—"this baby's state of the art. Now, any time I get tired of one of my sugars . . ."—the driver reached inside one of the plastic protectors directly overhead and slid out a photo— "I just slide her out." Rolling down the window, he held the photo into the car's slipstream but didn't let go—". . . toss her, and put me up a new one."

Saying that, he carefully replaced the photo. Lane watched him pat it lovingly.

"Don't you worry none, Trudy honey," the driver said to the girl as he patted the picture, "I wasn't gonna throw you away yet." He turned to Lane flashing him his shit-eating grin. "Hell of a lot cheaper than buying a new car. Am I right?"

Lane nodded. The driver grinned back.

Then he suddenly broke into snorts of laughter.

"Got me a confession to make," he told Lane. "I was pulling your leg a mite. Ain't my car. It's a friend's. I'm just returning it to him." He noticed the look of relief on Lane's face. "Had you going, didn't I?"

The driver extended his hand.

"Name's Goodall. Bob Goodall."

"Lane Dixon," Lane said, shaking, though not so sure he wanted to be on a first-name basis with the driver.

"Where you headed, Lane?"

"Utah," he said guardedly.

"Big damn place, Utah."

"Salt Lake City," Lane returned after a beat.

The driver looked at him and smiled. "Me too. How's that for luck? First I save you from freezing to death out there on the road, and now you got yourself a free ride to Mormonland."

Lane managed a weak smile. "Must be my lucky day."

"Must be. Almost didn't stop. In the old days I'd never think twice of picking up a rider, but these days you can't be too careful who you let in your car."

"Something wrong?" Lane asked. Bob had fallen silent and begun to regard Lane with sharp, probing stares.

"No. Just that for a moment there . . . well, you kinda reminded me of someone."

Bob kept staring hard at Lane, who turned to look out the window to avoid his piercing gaze.

Superimposed over his own reflection in the glass, he saw Bob still staring at him. It was making him uncomfortable. He wished he could get out.

Then, almost like the answer to a prayer, Lane spotted a billboard coming up. It advertised a restaurant/bar just three miles down the road, the Pick 'n' Drill Bar.

"You know," he said, turning back to Bob and trying to sound offhanded, "if you'd just let me out at this place coming up, that'd be great."

"I thought you were heading to Utah."

"Well, I forgot," he answered, this time knowing it sounded lame. "I, uh, need to make a call."

The cowboy studied Lane for a long second, then stared back out the windshield at the dark road ahead.

"I don't think so," he said in an even voice, not smiling anymore. Lane felt the Caddy accelerate. "There's another place 'bout twenty miles—"

"Look, I said I want out *here*," Lane returned, his voice rising.

"Sorry friend. This here's mining country," the driver answered. "It's a Friday night. In these parts, that's about the same as a full moon in Transylvania."

"I can take care of myself."

The cowboy eyed Lane appraisingly. The hitchhiker was wiry and he looked strong. But he was only semitough as far as the good-old-boys in these parts went. The driver knew he wouldn't last five seconds in a fight. Make that three.

"You know, I believe you might just be stupid enough to try," he said to Lane.

The Caddy had eaten up the miles, and the place up ahead swam into the glare of the high-brights. Less than a minute and they'd have already passed it by. Lane watched the bar come steadily nearer. He stared the driver straight in the eye.

"Look, goddammit. I don't want out at the next town. So stop the damn car!" His tone was a flat don't-screw-with-me order.

The cowboy studied Lane's face.

He didn't see a trace of fear in it.

With a slight nod, as if he'd made up his mind about something, he lightened up on the accelerator and reached beneath the dash, turning off the Caddy's interior light.

Seconds later, he pulled in front of the bar

and stopped. Lane climbed out and took his pack out of the rear.

The Pick 'n' Drill was little more than an unpainted shack, its entrance lit by a single naked bulb.

If it hadn't been for the dozen or so cars and pickups parked in front and to either side, and the slithery sound of steel guitars coming from the jukebox inside, it could have passed for any of the ghost buildings that dotted the county.

Lane turned toward the entrance when the driver's voice stopped him.

"Hey, son," he said.

Lane stopped and looked back.

"If I was you, I'd try not to act like John Wayne in there."

"Thanks for the lift," Lane said, and turned back toward the entrance.

Behind him he heard the scream of tire rubber being laid down as the big Caddy peeled off onto the highway and was swallowed up by the black desert night.

Behind the wheel of the Caddy, the driver's eyes scanned the image quickly receding in the rearview mirror.

His passenger looked even more alone now than he'd seemed back there on the road. He couldn't help feeling sorry for the dude.

What he was about to experience in there would likely be pure hell.

"Damn," he said to himself. "Lettin' a bunch of naked women scare you off."

The cowboy shook his head morosely and flipped on the radio.

As the steel guitars came on with their familiar wail, his eyes reflexively went back to the mirror.

But there was nothing there anymore. Only the blackness.

Only the emptiness of the road behind him.

4

Lane pushed through the ramshackle door and went into the roadhouse. From the appearance of the building, Lane hadn't expected the Ritz. He hadn't expected much more than the car he'd just fled. Even so, the Pick 'n' Drill was a lot worse-looking inside than he'd imagined it could be.

The dim, drafty dive occupied a single room about fifty feet square. It stank of sweat, stale cigarette smoke, and other things Lane didn't want to think about. The wood-plank floors ran the length of the room and were covered with sawdust.

Loud country-western music blared from the jukebox tucked away in a corner. Three couples danced nearby. There was a bar at the back, at which a handful of local boys sat drinking. A game of pool took place in the center, with about a dozen cowboys clustered around it.

By the time Lane reached the bar, the pool

game had come to a sudden stop. Lane felt eyes boring into his back but kept his body language nonchalant.

The bartender was a mammoth guy with greasy locks of his long black hair falling lankily from under his cowboy hat. He eyed Lane but didn't make a move to serve him as Lane bellied up to the bar.

"Howdy. I'll have a beer," Lane said to him.

"Don't have beer," the bartender answered back. From the scowl on his face the guy obviously wasn't trying to be funny.

Lane looked around him. The room was full of local boys and their dates, most holding long-necked brown bottles of the local microbrew.

"Okay. Then I'll have whatever's in those bottles."

The bartender hesitated a moment. Then he took a beer from the cooler and set it in front of Lane. The bartender quickly took Lane's money as a bunch of pool players moved toward him.

Lane sipped at his beer and, turning to the bartender, said, "I was hoping I might catch a ride into Raton."

A tall, wiry man with big hands set his pool cue carefully down on the bar, next to Lane.

"Well, you might be waiting here a long time, then," he said.

"I'd take a ride anywhere in that direction," Lane replied.

"Yeah," the guy said with a snicker, "I just bet you would."

Lane heard the snide laughter but ignored the crude put-down. He wasn't afraid of the guy, and he wasn't about to let himself get pushed around.

"You have a problem with something?" he told him.

The pool player didn't answer Lane. Instead he looked back at a smaller man standing directly behind him. He then motioned for the other guy to step forward.

When the small man got up close, Lane saw that his hands were bandaged and his face badly bruised. It looked like somebody had whaled on him pretty good.

"You say this is the guy, Ben?" the pool player asked him.

"Yeah. He's one of 'em, all right, Rick."

Ben glared daggers at Lane.

"My friend, Ben, here"—the pool-player looked down at the table as if to line up a shot, then back up at Lane—"was in Raton last Friday night and claims you and some of your friends jumped him."

"He's mistaken," Lane answered.

"And you're a goddamn liar!" Ben hollered, taking a belligerent step toward Lane.

The pool player stretched out his long arm

and held the smaller guy back. Lane caught sight of one of the couples by the jukebox, heading toward the door.

It didn't take an Einstein to know that some bad shit was about to hit the fan. Lane half-rose in his seat and called after them.

"Hey, how about a—"

"Ride?" the pool player finished for him, shoving him back with his pool cue as the couple disappeared out the door and went for their pickup. "They aren't going in your direction. 'Course, right now I figure you'd probably take a lift in any direction."

If Lane was afraid, he didn't show it as he shot the pool player a level gaze.

"Look, I'm not calling your friend or anybody else a liar. All I'm saying is I wouldn't have done that to anybody."

Rick moved the tip of the pool cue off Lane's chest. He nodded understandingly but said nothing, and Lane reached for his beer.

At the same instant, Rick grabbed the pool cue and in a short, fast, vicious stroke, knocked the bottle clean off the bar and sent it crashing to the floor.

Lane already saw the cue swinging at his gut as he reacted to the play, but by then it was too late. The tip stabbed his solar plexus.

Lane collapsed onto the sawdust-strewn floor. He half-rolled, clutching his abdomen. It felt like the wind had been cut out of him.

"You made a real bad mistake comin' in here," the pool player growled, looking down at Lane, then he handed the cue to another man.

"Now, seein' as Ben can't do this to you himself," he added as he shrugged off his jacket, "I'm gonna teach you a lesson."

Lane felt himself hauled roughly off the floor by two cowboys who set him up like a scarecrow on a stake. The pool player smiled at him for a second. Then he let go with a hammering uppercut to Lane's jaw.

"Your memory becoming any clearer, boy?" he asked.

"I . . . I never saw him before," Lane managed to croak out as the room swam.

The pool player shook his head and wound up his fist for another shot at Lane's face. But before he could unload the bomber, Lane drew up his knees and kicked like a mule, catching him in the gut and knocking Rick back over the table behind him.

The sudden movement also loosened the grips of the two cowboys holding him down, allowing Lane to slip free of one of them and bang his ugly face with a short, poleaxing right that made blood spurt from the guy's broken septum.

As Lane blocked a clumsy, telegraphed left from the other guy, three more cowboys came hustling to their buddies' rescue.

Lane found himself pinioned again as the pool player staggered up from the floor. The pool player's hair and clothes covered with sawdust and his eyes wet and huge with boiling rage.

"Son ... of ... a ... *bitch*!" he hollered. "Get his goddamn legs!"

One of the cowboys knelt down and got a two-handed lock on Lane's legs. He wouldn't be doing any more mule-kicking for a while, that was a fact.

When this was taken care of, the pool player took a quick step forward and drilled a left-right combination into Lane's gut with punishing force. Lane hung there like meat on a hook.

The pool player wiped sweat off his brow and turned to a big, muscular Indian wearing a beat-up army jacket, standing at the bar. The name *Lucas* was stenciled in black over the jacket's right pocket.

"I got to take a leak," the pool player said to the Indian. "Luke, you keep him warmed up till I get back."

The Indian pushed up the sleeves of his jacket over arms only slightly narrower than tree trunks as he crossed toward Lane.

The toilet stank of piss, but the pool player didn't mind. He already had his fly open and his pecker out.

When nature called, a man had to answer,

after all. And besides, he didn't want to waste a second on emptying his beer-distended bladder when there was some prime ass-kicking to be done out in the bar.

He was so intent on whaling on the punk that he didn't pay any mind to the fact that the bathroom's window was open and a pair of boots were visible through the bottom of the lone stall.

As he sidled up to the porcelain urinal and started to piss, he heard a loud thump come from beyond the door.

Damn that Luke, he thought as he relieved himself, *already starting in. Gotta finish quick before that Indian kills the sucker and takes away my Friday night entertainment.*

"Hey, Luke!" Rick shouted, loud enough to be heard through the crapper door. "I said don't kill the bastard till I get back! Hear?"

Forcing the last few dribbles of brew from his bladder, the pool player laughed out loud. He imagined his fist pounding the punk's face to sticky red jelly. Damn, he loved Friday nights.

Rick didn't hear the squeak of the stall door swinging out on its rusty hinges or see the cowboy, in a canhart jacket and Stetson hat pulled low over his eyes, bolt out of the stall.

The pool player only glimpsed the flash of the long, shiny blade of the coffin-handled knife, which the drunk had pulled from somewhere, before he banged his head against the toilet's graffiti-covered wall.

The pool player started to make a move, but the cold bite of the knife blade against his dick stopped him in a second flat.

"Try it and it's history," a voice told him matter-of-factly.

He looked into the take-no-shit eyes of the other man and knew that he could easily be doing the rest of his pissing through a plastic straw. This dude was not screwing with him. He meant it.

The pool player didn't move.

Luke had hardly broken a sweat.

But, then, he never did.

He'd already hit Lane with a few gentle love-taps. This time he was winding up for something a little less romantic.

A crowd of half-drunk good-old-boys stood around, throwing back beers and egging Luke on. Before Luke could hit Lane again, though, he heard the pool player's voice come from the crapper.

"Luke," Rick shouted. "Hey, man. Bring that guy in here. Alone, man."

There was something funny about the pool player's voice, Luke thought. Like he was afraid of something.

Luke was nobody's fool. He jerked his head at another Indian, who immediately went outside. Then, as Lane watched the Indian leave, Luke grabbed Lane with one coal-bucket-sized hand and reached across the bar with the other.

He held his hand open in front of the bartender.

"No way," the bartender told him, taking a step back.

"Way," the Indian said, and snapped his fingers. There was not the slightest bit of humor in his remark. It was an order.

The bartender knew he had no other choice, unless he wanted to take Lane's place. He sullenly reached under the bar and brought up an old Colt .38 revolver. He slipped the piece into Luke's waiting hand.

Holding the wheel gun close against his thigh, the Indian flipped the cylinder catch and found all six bullets in their notches. He started for the toilet with Lane in tow.

At the same time, the other Indian, who'd gone outside, crept silently up to the open rest-room window. Standing on an upended milk crate, he cautiously peered inside, just able to make out the pool player's hands raised on top of his head.

The Indian could see nothing else at first, just the top of his buddy Rick's head, but a picture was worth a thousand words. He waited a while longer. Then they moved a little and he saw the knife. He sized up the situation and knew what he had to do when the time came.

"Luke, you asshole! Get him in here!"

The first Indian was already halfway to the toilet by this point. The pool player didn't have to paint him a picture. Somebody was in there with him.

But by now Joe was in position out back. The trace of a smile flitted across Luke's mean, angular face. The play would be tight and fast. But it would go down all right.

"Okay, man!" Luke hollered back to Rick. "Don't panic. We're coming!"

The second Indian went to one of the pick-ups parked outside and reached under the tarp that covered the cargo bed.

He brought out a .30–.30 lever-action Remington.

Cartridges were already loaded, ready for chambering.

Quietly closing the door, he stepped to the rest room's open window and raised the rifle to his shoulder.

Sighting down the barrel, he saw that he didn't have a clear shot yet.

But that was okay.

It would come.

*   *   *

Luke took a deep breath and kicked open the crapper door. He jammed the muzzle of the Colt into Lane's right temple.

"Okay, man," he said to the cowboy holding the pool player. "Let him go or I'll blow your friend's head right off."

For emphasis, he cocked the hammer and jammed the gun into Lane's ear. The man behind the pool player changed position, and for the first time, Lane got a good look at the face under the brim of the cowboy hat.

It was Bob Goodall, the guy he'd hitched the ride with. For some reason he couldn't fathom, Lane wasn't too surprised.

"Some friends you got," Goodall said to the pool player in a deadpan voice, then, to Luke, "I didn't come to negotiate, pal."

The pool player's eyes bulged in their sockets with fear.

"Don't bargain with him, you asshole! He'll cut my dick off!" His voice was shrill. His cool was totally blown.

Bob locked eyes with the Indian, and a silent wave of understanding passed between them. They were two of a kind, and they both knew it.

The Mexican standoff ended when, after a long moment, Luke thumbed the Colt's hammer back in place and lowered the gun.

"Now let him go and slide that piece over here," Bob told him.

Luke pushed Lane away from him and into

the bathroom. Bob ignored Lane, keeping his attention riveted on the gun as Luke put it on the floor and kicked it toward Bob.

"Pick it up," Bob told Lane. "Hold it on him."

Lane did as he was told, wincing in pain.

"You okay?" Bob asked.

Lane nodded.

"Come over here and get the car keys out of my pockets," Bob added.

Lane reached into Bob's jacket and dug out the keys to the Caddy.

"Back the car up to the door and, when you're ready, honk once." Bob looked back at Luke.

Lane asked, "What about you?"

"I'll be out directly," he said with a grin.

Outside, Lane spotted the Caddy parked in the shadows beyond the perimeter of dull yellow light cast by the building's naked bulb. He moved toward the car, fighting back the pain of the beating he'd taken inside.

"Hey, man," the pool player told Bob, back in the toilet. "He let the guy go. Why don't you do likewise. That was the deal, right?"

"Deal? Who said anything about a deal?" Bob answered flatly, keeping his stare fixed on Luke. The pool player looked down in horror.

"What're you goin' to do?" he asked pleadingly.

Neither man could see the second Indian

outside the open window. He had a good shot now, and he fingered the trigger as, despite the fierce cold, beads of sweat stood poised on his brow.

The pool player let out a high-pitched, womanish scream as Bob made a sudden, swift cutting motion with the knife. The pool player grabbed for his crotch between his legs as Bob turned toward the Indian and held out his clenched fist. But when he opened it, his hand was empty.

Bob grinned broadly at Luke, but the Indian stared at him impassively.

He wasn't impressed.

But, then again, it wasn't Luke's dick that had hung in the balance. It was the pool player's. And Rick had collapsed against the graffiti-covered crapper wall, knowing the bliss of those who had found religion.

"You still itchin' for a fight?" Bob challenged the Indian. "Come on, then. Let's do it!"

Nobody moved, though. Not the pool player. Not the Indian.

Bob caught the way Luke's eyes flicked to the open window, though, and suddenly realized that he was exposed in the center of the room.

The Lord never created a more perfect target, Bob knew, than he was at that moment.

At the same instant, he heard the telltale

ratcheting of a bullet being cranked into a rifle's firing chamber. There was no way he could do anything before the bullet drilled through the back of his head. Bob knew he'd blown it. He was already toast.

A second passed, though, then another. Bob wondered why the hell he was still alive.

Then he heard Lane's voice from outside.

"Bob! It's okay," Lane was shouting as he held the .38 pressed hard against the small of the second Indian's back.

Less than five minutes after Bob had pulled open the door on the run and jumped inside, with Lane behind the Caddy's wheel, they were hauling ass away from the bar with every ounce of torque the white chariot could deliver to its steel-radial tires.

Riding high on a rush of adrenaline, Bob was going through the giddiness of what soldiers know as post-combat euphoria. Laughing uncontrollably, Bob flung his cowboy hat into the back seat.

"Goddamn!" he shouted. "Whoo-eee! Nothing like a little excitement to get the ol' blood a'pumpin' and—" He stopped short as he saw Lane check the rearview. "What're you looking for?"

"Them."

"Somebody following us?" he said calmly, looking back out the rear windshield.

"Not yet."

"That's 'cause it takes a few minutes to change a flat tire," Bob said, and slipped his knife back into the sheath in his boot. He sat up and grinned.

"You slashed their tires?"

"Hell, no," Bob returned. "I'd have been there all night."

"Then what . . ."

Bob was reaching into the pocket of his down vest. When he pulled out his hand and opened his palm, Lane saw a handful of tire valve stems.

Lane exhaled slowly.

Nobody would be following them now, he knew, and eased up on the gas pedal. With a snort of laughter, Bob shucked off his jacket and flung it into the back to join his hat.

"How you feeling? You must'a got worked over pretty good."

"I'll live, thanks," Lane answered, seeing genuine concern in Bob's eyes. Bob smiled at Lane and settled back into his seat.

"Feeling's mutual, pardner."

5

Sheriff Buck Olmstead sat at his desk reading the fax that had come in a few minutes ago.

He glanced at the clock on the other desk beside him. Its digital face showed the time as 4:45 A.M.

Damn computers, he thought.

No way any human being fed a sheet of paper into a fax machine at this hour, even considering where the fax had just come from. Olmstead didn't look up as Nate came into the office, heading straight for Olmstead's electric coffeemaker.

"Heard you were in early," Nate said, pouring himself a waxed-paper cupful. "Forensics found a hair in that second bed. They're pushing it through." He put down the carafe and took a sip. "We've also isolated twenty unknowns in those tapes."

Olmstead didn't answer his deputy. He was preoccupied with the fax in front of him. Nate studied the top of the sheriff's head for a long beat as he took another slug of the coffee.

"Ran into Billy Coogan last night," Nate went on, although Olmstead still wasn't looking at him. "Say's you're leading McGinnis two-to-one out this way."

Olmstead finally laid down the fax and looked up at Nate, who could tell at a glance that Olmstead hadn't heard a single word he'd said.

"Did you end up calling in the Fed boys on the motel killings?" he wanted to know.

"No. Why?"

Olmstead held up the fax by the corners. Nate saw the logo of the Federal Bureau of Investigation at the top of the page. He couldn't see much else. But then again, he didn't need to.

" 'Cause it looks like we've got company," Olmstead said.

Frank LaCrosse watched the morgue attendant pull the two drawers from the wall. Inside each was a body.

The morgue attendant matched the tag numbers of the cadavers against those on the computer printout in his hand. Satisfied they were the right decedents, he stepped back to let the FBI agent inspect them.

Frank had already snapped on a pair of thin latex gloves and now went to work examining the two cadavers. He did so with a clinical detachment that went with his straight, regular features and the camel-wool topcoat worn over the dark suit, all of which J. Edgar Hoover would have readily approved.

"You ever seen anything like that before?" asked the morgue attendant as LaCrosse finished his examination and began removing his rubber gloves.

The FBI man regarded the morgue attendant dispassionately for a long second.

"Yes," he said.

At five in the morning Davie's Diner was packed with cops. The regulars. They filled the window booths that looked out on the boulevard, the tables scattered between them and the counter, and the counter itself.

Thirty years in the business and Davie's hadn't been held up once. Went with the territory.

Olmstead and Nate sat at one of the booths opposite Jim Shawcroft, a State Highway Patrol captain. Shawcroft, in a long raincoat, was telling Olmstead a joke, which, at Davie's, meant he was also telling the rest of the diner the joke, since pretty much everybody else was within earshot.

Shawcroft's partner, Hank Miller, stared out the window, looking at the snow. He'd heard the joke before.

"So I get to the scene and there's a tour bus

on its side in this field," Shawcroft said in the middle of his story. "Thirty, forty people dead, and running around the bus is this damn chimpanzee. So I walk over to Miller, and I say, 'What happened?' Well, I'll be damned if that monkey didn't come over and start going like this. . . ." Shawcroft pantomimed drinking.

"So Miller says, 'Jim, I think he's trying to tell you something.' So I look at that monkey and say, 'You telling me folks on this bus were drinking?' The monkey nods, then he started doing this. . . ."

Now Shawcroft did the wing part of a buck-and-wing, raising one of his fingers in a Cab Calloway hi-dee-ho.

"I said, 'Dancin'! They were drinking *and* dancin'?' So now the monkey nods and starts doing this. . . ."

The door to Davie's opened as Shawcroft began unbuttoning his shirt and pantomiming a hootchy-kootchy dance. Frank LaCrosse entered the diner and spoke to a young deputy seated at the counter. Olmstead watched the deputy nod his way as Shawcroft continued his story.

"Well, I looked at Miller and said, 'Why, hell! No wonder that bus crashed. They were drunk and dancing and every mother's one of 'em buck naked.' So finally I looked at that monkey and said, 'You know you were awful damn lucky to come out of there alive. What were you doing all that time?' And the monkey goes. . . ."

Raising both his hands, Shawcroft made like he was driving and looking over his shoulder goggle-eyed.

Every single patron in Davie's Diner broke up laughing. Even the otherwise sullen Miller cracked a half-smile.

Then Shawcroft saw LaCrosse coming toward them and stopped smiling. The guy had the word *Fed* written all over him. He nudged Miller and put on his hat. Both troopers got up to leave.

"See ya, Buck," Shawcroft said before walking away. "Good luck today."

"Thanks Jim," Olmstead returned. "Be careful out there. And don't forget to stop by the polls."

Shawcroft nodded at LaCrosse and went out the door with Miller in train just as the waitress brought over Olmstead and Nate's breakfast. She set down the plates and a check and started off.

"Sheriff Olmstead?" LaCrosse asked, coming abreast of the table. For the moment Olmstead decided he'd ignore him.

"Sally?"

"It's coming, Sheriff," she called back, and grabbed a bottle of ketchup off the counter, setting it in front of the plates. After all these years she knew Olmstead pretty well. Spotting the newcomer standing beside the sheriff, the waitress figured she might as well take his order and pulled out her pad and pen.

"How about some breakfast, Mr. LaCrosse," said Olmstead.

"No, thank you," LaCrosse returned. Olmstead noticed it was matter-of-fact. No smile. No inflection. Only a politeness without warmth or humor.

LaCrosse shook his head at the waitress. "No thanks," he told her, and took a seat at a vacant counter stool across from the booth Olmstead and Nate occupied.

"And what can we do for the FBI today?" said Olmstead, glancing down and noticing LaCrosse's spit-shined brown wing-tip Oxfords.

"You've got two bodies in the morgue," returned LaCrosse. "I need the car that was taken from the motel."

"Take a number," Olmstead said, slopping ketchup onto his scrambled eggs, "and get in line."

"Time is critical, Sheriff."

Olmstead set down the ketchup bottle and screwed its cap back on. "Time is always critical, Mr. LaCrosse. What makes you so sure we're talking about the same killer?" Olmstead put a forkful of shirred eggs into his mouth and chewed.

"Severed femoral artery. Single incisions." LaCrosse's monotonic delivery shocked Olmstead. It was like he was a computer spitting out data. "Five to seven inches long," he went on. "Inch to inch and a half deep."

"You saw the bodies?"

"No prints," LaCrosse went on in the same monotone. "No weapon. No witnesses."

Olmstead set down his fork and looked hard at LaCrosse. The full implication of what the Fed was telling him had finally sunk in. LaCrosse's next words confirmed Olmstead's thoughts.

"I know this killer, Sheriff. When he kills he hits the road and he moves fast, and the only chance you have of finding him is finding what he's driving or being incredibly lucky."

For the first time Olmstead noticed that the whole place had gone as quiet as a cloister on the moon. Every cop in the place was watching the exchange. Leaning back, Olmstead kept his voice level.

"You mind if I call you by your first name, Frank?"

Buck continued without waiting for a reply. "Frank, you say you know this killer?" Olmstead returned. "You got a physical description? Height? Weight?"

"We believe him to be a male between the ages of twenty and fifty. Medium to large build. From the western United States but having spent considerable time in the east."

Olmstead forced a half-smile.

"That really narrowed the field, Frank."

"He's a serial killer, Sheriff."

"The serial killers we've dealt with don't seem to want their victims found," Nate added.

LaCrosse turned and looked Nate straight in the eye.

"This one does."

"Why?"

LaCrosse looked down for a second.

"I don't know," he said.

Just then Olmstead noticed a sheriff's department car pulling up in the diner's parking lot. He turned from LaCrosse and signaled the waitress.

"Sally, a cup to go, please."

Nate scarfed the rest of his breakfast and slid a half-eaten danish wrapped in a napkin into his pocket. He knew Olmstead well—well enough to know when a meal on the job was over.

The young deputy who'd climbed out of the car came through Davie's door and caught Olmstead's eye. They quickly exchanged words in hushed tones. Something had broken in the case and everybody in the diner knew it.

"Well, Frank," Olmstead said as he put on his hat, "maybe we'll both get lucky today."

*　*　*

The red Ford Explorer sat abandoned in front of the four-story apartment building in downtown Amarillo. City police vehicles lined the street.

It was still dark out, but even so, there was a sizeable civilian turnout as well. Local residents hung out of windows and rubberneckers stood on the sidewalk.

Olmstead already knew that McGinnis had set up a command post near the building; and as his car pulled up, he could see McGinnis standing by an Amarillo police car positioned close to the action. Olmstead got out with LaCrosse. They were met by a deputy sheriff who briefed them on their way to the command post.

"City police spotted the car about four A.M.," said the deputy. "Officials tailed it here. Instead of waiting for backup, one of the cops followed him inside and the suspect began shooting."

"Wonderful," Olmstead said in disgust.

"McGinnis got his SWAT team in there now," the deputy went on. "He won't let any of our people near the place."

"Course not. The television trucks might pull up any moment," Olmstead answered dryly.

As the sheriff moved toward McGinnis's

command post, LaCrosse walked around the building and went to the Explorer.

Borrowing a Maglite from one of Olmstead's deputies, LaCrosse shone the powerful beam of the tactical flashlight through the windows of the car. Nothing.

He switched off the Maglite and tucked it under his arm.

The latch of the driver's side door had been extended. LaCrosse pulled open the door and climbed inside. Using the Maglite, he subjected the interior to a careful inspection.

Again there was nothing. LaCrosse then felt under the seats. His fingers nudged a small, smooth object. When he picked it up, he saw that it was a cheap wallet of dyed black cowhide.

Opening the wallet and inspecting its contents, LaCrosse noted that it contained no cash or driver's license.

It did, however, contain a miscellaneous assortment of credit cards, most of them in the name of one William Suderland.

LaCrosse made a mental note of the name, replaced the cards, and pocketed the wallet.

He had put his hand on the door handle, meaning to leave, when he suddenly began to sniff the air.

6

"Well, Buck,"—McGinnis smiled at the sheriff as he came up to the command post. McGinnis held a compact two-way radio in his hand; he'd been using it when Olmstead approached—"Came to see how a real operation is done?"

"I declare, Jack. You must have calluses from patting yourself on the back all the time How about just giving me the facts?"

McGinnis was dour. "We've got him on the third floor. Trying to talk him out."

LaCrosse ran his hands down the side of the back seat. He was searching for the seat release so he could get into the back of the Explorer. He finally found it, but it was stuck.

"Hold that," he said to the deputy who stood outside the car, handing him the flash.

While the deputy trained the light through the window, LaCrosse used both hands to drop the rear seat. It fought him for a minute.

Then, with a hard pull, it dropped down with a snap and a clunk.

A dead man's head and shoulders were suddenly exposed. There was a single bullet hole through the forehead, lined with congealed blood.

The deputy dropped the light and gagged.

"Jesus!" he groaned, fighting the urge to retch against the side of the car.

Now a crowd was beginning to gravitate toward the vehicle. Other cops and rubberneckers had seen what had happened. These included Olmstead and McGinnis.

"What the hell's going on over there?" McGinnis asked.

Before he or Olmstead could make a move, a series of sharp, rapid reports broke the morning stillness.

"Bill!" McGinnis shouted as he keyed the radio and shouted to the leader of his SWAT team.

The voice came back instantly. Tense. Afraid. Angry.

The firing continued.

McGinnis and Olmstead could both hear it over the radio.

"Christ! Allen's down! We can't reach him. Shit! We're falling back!"

Suddenly it stopped and there was nothing.

"Bill? Bill? . . ." McGinnis shouted into the communicator unit.

"I'm okay," the SWAT leader returned after a long pause. "Allen's hit. He's in the hall. Need instructions. Over."

Beads of sweat stood out on McGinnis's face. His eyes had a wild look. He knew every cop in the vicinity had their eyes on him. Watching. Listening. Waiting to see how he'd handle the situation. Waiting for him to tell them what to do.

But McGinnis had frozen. The gears of his mind had ground to a complete stop. It was a machine that refused to function. The Amarillo city police chief's glance fell on Olmstead. There was a pleading look in his eyes now.

"Get him out, Jack," Olmstead said.

McGinnis licked his lips. All his former cockiness was gone. For a moment he began to say something.

A man in a camel-wool coat appeared out of the twilight and stood beside Olmstead.

"Is he alone?"

The effect of LaCrosse's voice was like an electric shock to McGinnis, jolting him back to reality. A calculating look came into his eyes.

"Who the hell's this?" he snapped at Olmstead.

"This is Frank LaCrosse," Olmstead replied. "FBI."

LaCrosse calmly addressed McGinnis again. "Ask him," he repeated.

"Listen mister. I've got a man down in there—"

"*Ask him!*"

It wasn't a request this time, both McGinnis and Olmstead both knew that. It was an order.

Instead of answering back, McGinnis keyed the commo unit and did what LaCrosse wanted.

"Bill, is he alone?"

"Can't tell," the SWAT leader's strained voice came back. "He says he's holding a knife on somebody."

Now they heard the crying of a child coming from the radio's speaker grille.

Before McGinnis noticed that he'd even gone, LaCrosse had started toward the building and had already crossed the street. The FBI man was already through the front entranceway before McGinnis's deputies could do anything to stop him.

McGinnis cursed and keyed the radio again.

"Bill, you're about to have some company," he said into the unit. "Stop him."

Holding the 9mm Sig Sauer P226 in a modified combat grip, LaCrosse mounted the internal stairway. He ascended sideways, back against the wall, to narrow his profile as much as possible.

Cops in the black ninja-suits of the Amarillo city Special Weapons and Tactics unit, armed with shotguns and Heckler-Koch MP5 sub-machine guns, were spaced out on the stairs.

LaCrosse put one finger to his lips as he passed them on his way up. Nobody said anything. Nobody moved.

Reaching the third floor landing, the Fed stopped abreast of the SWAT-team leader. The kid's crying filled the hallway, echoing off the walls. LaCrosse's eyes moved along the hallway beyond the landing and saw the cop who'd been hit by gunfire. He lay bleeding from a severe stomach wound, already lapsing into shock from the looks of things.

Suddenly there was a shout from the open door of an apartment a few yards down the hall from the wounded cop. The voice was hoarse from shouting, wound tight by adrenaline, crazed, desperate; the voice of a man on the edge and about to go over.

"Shut that kid up," shouted the voice. "Get her in there and shut the door!"

LaCrosse's voice was controlled and crisp as he addressed the SWAT leader.

"Only one down?"

"Yeah," the cop whispered. "But, sir. Chief McGinnis said . . ."

LaCrosse was already on his way to the open doorway of the apartment before the other man could finish speaking. He had other things on his mind.

"Shit," the SWAT leader said into his comm unit. "He's going into the room!"

Outside, McGinnis took the radio from the side of his face and put it in his coat pocket.

He looked hard at Olmstead.

"If that son-of-a-bitch gets one of my men killed . . ." he began.

"Then you'd look pretty bad, Jack," Olmstead told him with a smile. "All this TV coverage and you in charge." Olmstead shook his head. "Yeah, you'd look real bad, Jack."

McGinnis looked around at the arriving trucks bearing television remote crews. Olmstead turned his glance from McGinnis toward the apartment house.

The arms of the SWAT leader reached out to take the wounded cop from LaCrosse, who had dragged him back along the hall. Already pumped up on his own brain chemicals, the fugitive became more manic when he heard the noise from outside the apartment.

"Who's out there!" he bellowed. "I swear to God I'll start cutting in here!"

The child's crying got louder as LaCrosse crossed toward the open doorway, where he stopped, reharnessed the Sig Sauer, and stepped into the room, surprising the man with the eight-inch bowie knife sitting in the corner and holding the edge of the blade to the throat of another man in front of him.

"Who the fuck are you?" shouted the knife-wielder. "I said I negotiate only by radio."

LaCrosse wasn't focusing on the man with the knife. His situation was static, contained for the moment—the spent Smith and Wesson .38 pistol lay at his feet. If he'd possessed another firearm, he'd be using it instead of the knife, LaCrosse reasoned.

"Hey, man, I'm talking to you!"

The FBI man's situational awareness was intent on absorbing the total picture. The knife-wielder was only a part of it.

LaCrosse wanted to know how big a part and what other elements comprised the overall tactical scenario before he dealt with the man in front of him.

He now focused his attention on the sound of the crying child. It was coming from a connecting room, through the closed doorway to his immediate right.

"Answer me!"

LaCrosse didn't. He stepped toward the closed door, focusing most of his attention on the sounds from the room beyond.

"Are you blind, man? I got a knife!"

LaCrosse half-turned his head. The knife-wielder was pressing the bowie blade into the soft, fatty tissue on the underside of his hostage's throat.

"I see it," was all LaCrosse replied.

Turning his head, he opened the bedroom door. A woman holding a child was huddled in one corner. LaCrosse held out his hands, gesturing for them to approach him.

LaCrosse then stepped back and guided them into the front room through the connecting doorway.

"No fuckin' way!" the knife-wielder shouted as they came through. "They go anywhere, I'm gonna cut him!"

"They don't have a choice," LaCrosse said softly, and by this time they were already at the door.

A split second later, they were out in the hallway.

It had happened in a flash. So quickly that the knife-wielder couldn't believe his eyes.

"I don't know who you are, you fucker, but I'm gonna make you pay," the guy with the blade threatened.

Through the doorway, LaCrosse saw the woman and the child hustled down the stairs by members of the SWAT team. Turning back into the room, he unholstered the Sig Sauer in a smooth, unbroken draw, cocking the action and chambering a parabellum round.

"Before you do, I have a question for you," LaCrosse said, stepping forward.

"A question?" the perp answered in a shout of anger. "I ain't answering none of your motherfucking ques—"

The bullet that augured into the doer's upper thigh at close range caused immediate hydrostatic shock as its kinetic energy was dispersed along the wound channel.

Trauma to the nervous system caused the knife-wielder to reflexively open his hand.

The wounded man looked at LaCrosse with a stunned expression as the knife clattered to the floorboards and the hostage broke free and ran out the door. The wounded man slid off the chair and onto the floor, crying out in agonizing pain.

Kneeling down beside him, LaCrosse flipped open the wallet he'd retrieved from the Explorer and held it open.

"Where did you get the car?" he asked.

"The car?" he answered. LaCrosse knew that shock was beginning to set in. He would have to act quickly to elicit the necessary information.

"The car from the motel," LaCrosse repeated. "Where did you get it?"

"I don't . . . know what you're . . . talking about. N-need a doctor."

LaCrosse asked the doer again as he showed him the wallet he'd found in the Explorer.

"I-I don't know nothing about no motel," stammered the perp. "I boosted it . . . b-boosted it this morning. Get me a doctor, man!"

"Where?" Frank shouted.

Before the bad actor could answer, two SWAT members rushed into the room. La-Crosse holstered the Sig Sauer.

He'd just run out of Q-and-A time.

The wounded man said nothing more as the SWAT team hustled him out of the room.

The TV camera crews were getting plenty of good footage as McGinnis's ninjas brought out the man whom LaCrosse had taken down for them.

McGinnis wasted no time in getting in on the action. It was he, after all, who had called in the media in the first place.

LaCrosse stayed in the background as Olmstead came up to him.

"Suderland's," LaCrosse said, handing him the wallet.

"Where'd you find it?"

"In the car. Along with the body."

Olmstead's head snapped up from the wallet. It took a second or two for what LaCrosse was telling him to register.

"Well, thank you, Frank," he answered finally, his voice dripping sarcasm. "Thirty-eight years of dedicated public service, and you came along and wiped the slate clean in one quick stroke."

"What's that supposed to mean?"

Olmstead looked away from LaCrosse. He realized he'd sounded off without any right.

He was out of line. If LaCrosse cracked the case, then so be it. Good for him.

"Nothing," Olmstead returned with a shrug. "I really am glad you caught the killer, Frank. I truly am."

LaCrosse's eyes left Olmstead's face. They focused on the injured hostage-taker, who was being examined by paramedics while TV cameras focused on the scene.

"He isn't the killer," LaCrosse said.

7

Lane Dixon was running from something. Something big. A roaring monstrosity that belched flame and smoke as it pursued him.

Lane risked a backward glance. It was a locomotive. A black locomotive painted with a grinning goblin's face. And it was gaining on him. Lane pumped his legs harder but still lost ground to the pursuing fiend. In only a second it would be on top of him, crushing him to jelly, reducing him to a smear.

Lane awoke with a start. A pretty girl, wearing nothing, looked him in the eye seeing nothing. She was one of the centerfold girls on the dash of Goodall's Caddy.

For a moment or two he felt disoriented, but then it all began to come back. Hitching a ride with Goodall. Then the trouble at the roadhouse. And finally passing the rest of the night inside Goodall's car.

Lane stretched and yawned. Where was Bob anyway? he asked himself. Probably out stretching his legs somewhere. Lane yawned again, realizing he was still half-asleep.

He wished he had a nice hot cup of black coffee right about now. That would do the trick.

Suddenly Lane felt something strange. It felt like the seat underneath him was vibrating.

At first he chalked it up to his imagination, but as the vibrations increased, Lane realized his mind had not been playing tricks on him.

The dashboard was vibrating too, and the girls' photos jiggled in their plastic mounts.

And there was also a deep rumbling noise all around him, much like the one he'd heard in his dream.

Lane was now wide awake. He wiped the fogged window with the sleeve of his jacket and looked out, his eyes widening in horror.

A diesel locomotive was speedballing straight at the car. It was only a few hundred yards away. In a matter of seconds Lane knew that it would be right on top of him.

The diesel blared its horn in warning as Lane clawed desperately at the buckle mechanism of his seat belt.

The entire Caddy was vibrating now, shaking like a leaf.

Lane felt his teeth chatter as he pulled the door handle and flung open the door.

The diesel horn blared again, this time with almost deafening loudness. Lane knew he only had a split instant to roll away from the doomed vehicle before the freight train plowed into it, reducing it to crumpled wreckage.

His life hanging by a thread, Lane flung himself out of the car.

He knew in his heart he wasn't going to make it.

The freight train screamed past the white Caddy like a juggernaut.

The car wasn't even touched.

Scrambling to his feet, Lane suddenly realized that he had never been in any danger at all. The car hadn't been parked on the tracks as he'd imagined, but less than a foot away.

Still too panicked to think clearly, Lane nevertheless realized instinctively that Bob had deliberately done this to him.

Lane heard a brash guffaw and turned. Bob stood by the tracks, answering the call of nature, as the line of boxcars and flatcars clattered past them.

"Your seven A.M. wake-up call, pardner."

Zipping his fly, Goodall walked back to the Caddy.

"Hey, you could have just given me a shake," Lane hollered at Bob, not knowing whether to be angry or plain grateful to still be alive. "I wake up easily."

Just then the last of the freight cars went

past, exposing what had been blocked from Lane's view.

"My God!" Lane said under his breath, his gaze riveted on a mesmerizing vision.

In the first light of day, the eastern wall of the Sangre de Cristo mountains rose to challenge the sky with an almost unearthly beauty.

The soaring peaks of black granite were capped with snow, which the wind swirled into feathery plumes that made the ice crystals give off scintillating rainbows in the light of the morning sun.

Lane had never seen the Rockies before. He stared at the mountains in awe, everything else forgotten.

Bob eyed his new friend with a knowing smile. He'd set everything up just to see the look on Lane's face at this moment.

"Hungry?" he asked.

Lane nodded. Both men climbed back into the car as the last rumble of the freight train echoed across the valley and finally died away.

Chief Jack McGinnis stood at the door of the conference room. He held a manila folder in his hand. It contained the rap sheet on the perp who'd been apprehended that morning in the apartment building.

He had a criminal history extending back

twelve years. The perp was an habitual offender, a real bad actor.

McGinnis had been reading off the stats to Olmstead, Nate, and LaCrosse, challenging their assertions that they had the wrong man. The perp was a bad-ass, sure, they claimed, but he wasn't the serial killer. No way.

"All I'm asking for is five minutes with him," LaCrosse pleaded with McGinnis.

"Five minutes?" McGinnis shouted back at him. "Hell, after what you did to him this morning, I'd probably be violating his civil rights allowing you in the same damn building with him!"

"That man is not the killer," LaCrosse repeated, not for the first time that day.

"You're sure about that, huh?"

"Absolutely," LaCrosse answered deadpanned.

"Buck?" McGinnis said to Olmstead after a moment or two of consideration. "You feel the same way?"

"He seems to know his man, Jack," Olmstead returned.

McGinnis nodded.

"Well, so do I," he said, and went back to the offender's rap sheet.

"Hector Saldez," he read. "Eight priors. Two assaults with a knife. Armed robbery. Conviction of second-degree murder in Oklahoma."

McGinnis closed the folder and handed it back to the uniformed cop with captain's bars standing beside him. The cop stood holding the folder in case McGinnis decided he wanted it again. "And now caught in possession of a murder victim's wallet and car," McGinnis summed up.

Olmstead and Nate traded glances. McGinnis had made his point. He had the stats to back his call. They only had LaCrosse's gut feel to go on. McGinnis's tactics might have been crude, but he'd managed to sandbag them just the same.

"Now you tell me again why you think this isn't the killer, Mr. LaCrosse," the chief said to the FBI man, leveling a stare at him.

LaCrosse's answer was calm and matter-of-fact.

"All you've got on him is possession of a stolen car," he said. "He didn't even know the wallet was there until I showed it to him. I bet he didn't even know there was a body in the trunk."

"Says you," McGinnis shot back. "Ballistics have already matched the gun he used on my men as the same one used to cap that John Doe in the car. Any more theories?"

Olmstead put in, "Jack, I think all Frank's saying is we have to keep our options open."

"There's no 'we' in this, Buck," McGinnis angrily shot back, his voice rising. "*I* have the suspect in custody and as soon as *I* get the green light from the D.A., *I'm* going to announce that Saldez is being charged with the murders of those three people."

McGinnis spun on his heels and headed for the door.

"Don't do that," LaCrosse said.

McGinnis stopped and turned to him.

"That bother you, Mr. LaCrosse?"

"He's setting you up," LaCrosse said. "You make that announcement, and he'll kill again just to embarrass you."

McGinnis screwed up his face in an expression of mocking contempt.

"Embarrass me?" he said. "I suppose you've had that happen to you before, Mr. LaCrosse."

"Yes," the FBI man returned, holding McGinnis's look. McGinnis tried but couldn't return the stare for long. Instead he turned to Olmstead, flashing his trademarked high-voltage smile.

"Oh, I get it now," McGinnis told him. "You'd like me to delay that announcement till after the election, wouldn't you, Buck? Nice try."

When he turned to walk out with the captain, McGinnis wasn't smiling anymore.

"Who the hell is this guy anyway?" he asked the captain. "I mean, how many times you seen an FBI agent work a case alone?"

They were already by the elevator. Mc-Ginnis pressed the down button. The numbers over the door began lighting up in red. The captain looked back at the conference room.

"We can find out," he said as the elevator arrived and they both got in.

LaCrosse stared out the conference-room window.

Olmstead and Nate traded glances, then Olmstead spoke up.

"Don't think much of us state and local boys, do you Frank?"

"It's a prejudice I have, Sheriff," LaCrosse returned. "No one's proved me wrong yet."

"You know, I don't think much of Jack either. It's not that I don't think he's a good cop, but he's a showboat. Yet, for a moment there, I found myself thinking he made a hell of a lot more sense than you."

"I don't care what you think, Sheriff," LaCrosse shot back, still staring at the snow, his back to Olmstead and Nate.

"Maybe not," Olmstead said back. "But you need me. Otherwise you'd be long gone by now."

LaCrosse turned and fixed Olmstead with an appraising stare. He paused a moment before speaking.

"Why believe me and not him?"

"Two reasons, Frank," Olmstead told him.

"First, I've seen a lot more murders than he has, and these don't seem to fit that man he's got in lockup. And second, in case you haven't noticed, Chief McGinnis and I are engaged in an election battle for my office, which he desperately wants and I, frankly, am desperate to defend."

LaCrosse was thunderstruck.

"Him? For sheriff?" he said. He shook his head as though he'd just heard a dirty joke with a lame ending.

"I'll take that as a compliment," Olmstead responded. "Fact remains, *he* has a suspect and *I* don't, and that makes me much more tolerant of dissenting opinions on who might have killed those folks. But I can't do anything to help unless I know what you know about this killer."

LaCrosse thought it over for a minute.

"Okay," he answered. "First we have to find John Doe's car."

"How the hell do you propose to do that when we don't even know who John Doe is?" Nate put in.

"We may not need to know," answered LaCrosse. "Start with where Saldez found Suderland's Explorer. That was the transfer point."

"McGinnis isn't going to let us within a hundred yards of Saldez," Nate challenged, shaking his head.

"Then go to his public defender," said LaCrosse.

"What makes you think he'll tell us, Frank?" Olmstead wanted to know.

"No way McGinnis will cut a deal with him right now," the Fed told him. "If he's innocent, he'll talk."

Olmstead thought about it, scratching his chin. He turned to Nate. "Make the call," he said.

"Then get a list of stolen vehicles and missing persons for the last two days," LaCrosse added.

"You got it," Nate told them. He got up and headed out the door. Olmstead watched him leave, then turned back to LaCrosse.

"I hope you're right about this, Frank," he said. "For both our sakes."

8

The Rockies were closer now.

Closer and even more impressive than they'd been on Lane's first sight of them.

Lane stared at the high peaks through the window of the roadside restaurant in which he and Bob Goodall sat, waiting to be served. Snow continued to fall steadily, lighter now than it had been on their way to the restaurant, but still coming down without any sign of letup.

Tiring of looking at the mountains, Lane idly watched an eighteen-wheeler pull into the truck-park beside the restaurant. Its driver, a big guy in a checkered mackinaw, climbed down from the running board and ambled toward the roadside diner.

His thoughts went back to the snow as the trucker passed out of view.

"How're we gonna get over with the storm?" he asked Bob who sat across from him.

Bob glanced out the window. "Ain't going to affect us much. It's moving north," he told him. Bob signaled the waitress, who called back that she'd be right over.

Lane flipped through the selections on the mini-jukebox to his right, not recognizing most of them. He guessed he wasn't much of a music lover.

"Last night," he said, turning back to Bob. "What made you come back?"

"Remember when I said you reminded me of someone? Well, you remind me of my little brother, Sam."

"Why?" Lane asked. "Does he get into jams like that too?"

"Used to," Bob replied. "He's dead now."

"Sorry," Lane said.

Bob changed the subject.

"I tell you, when I turned around and saw that old .30-.30 staring down at me," he said, "I thought 'This is it, Bob, no joining the birds this time.' "

"Joining what?"

"The birds," Bob answered. "Old railroaders used to say if you were on a train that was about to crash and you had a chance to jump that you were 'joinin' the birds.' "

"You worked on the railroad?" Lane asked.

"For a while. Mined awhile. Cowboy'd awhile. Fact is, I've done a little bit of everything up here," Bob concluded. "What about you, Lane Dixon? What kind of work you do?"

Lane looked away and spun the dial on the mini-juke again. Without meeting Bob's eyes, he replied, "I guess you could say I'm between jobs right now."

"And before that?" asked Goodall, not to be put off.

"Before that . . . I worked in a hospital."

"You an orderly?" asked Bob. "Nurse maybe?"

Lane kept spinning the mini-juke's dial. He'd seen all the songs before, but he wasn't really paying attention anyway.

"I did a little bit of everything," he finally answered.

Bob kept pressing Lane.

"That what's in Utah?" he asked. "A job?"

"No," Lane answered, finally looking back at Bob. "I've just been traveling. It's my first time west."

"West of what?" Bob wanted to know. "Denver? The Mississippi?"

"Philadelphia," Lane retorted, then shook his head and changed his mind. "No, that's not completely true. I've been out to California once."

He looked back out the window, into the snow that had thickened now to a heavy fall, and then past the snow into the Sangre de Cristo range beyond the roadway. "But looking down at the mountains from thirty-five thousand feet isn't quite the same as being there."

"True," Bob agreed, following Lane's gaze.

"All my life," Lane told him, holding the thought, "that's the way it's been. Safe. Calculated. Looking at life through a window. I thought it was time to see it differently."

"Well, pardner, you sure came to the right place," Bob answered with a smile and watched a guy in a grease-spattered apron, who had to be the place's cook, come over and clean a place at the counter next to their booth for the trucker Lane had seen climbing out of his rig.

A lull had fallen over Lane and Bob's conversation, and in it they both overheard the byplay from the counter.

"Come over from Salida?" the cook was asking the trucker.

"Uh-huh."

"How is it up there?" the cook wanted to know.

"Not bad," the trucker told him. "Worst of it's going north."

Lane looked at Bob and told him that his forecast about the snowstorm had been dead-on. He was impressed.

"Well, my father used to say that the weather don't make the rules, the mountains do," Bob answered. "And I know the mountains, pardner."

Just then the waitress Bob had signaled came by with a carafe of coffee. She was young and pretty, with a nice figure and a smile that lit up her face.

"How y'all doing?" she asked, filling their cups.

"We're doing just fine here," Bob told her, flashing her a broad smile.

"How 'bout you, darlin'?" she asked Lane. "Get you anything?"

Her smile told Lane that she might just mean something more than an omelette or a danish.

"No thanks," Lane told her, wanting to flirt with her but just not feeling up to it.

"Your friend's cute, but shy," the waitress told Bob.

"Hell, he just ain't used to looking at somebody as pretty as yourself is all," Bob sugared her back without missing a beat.

Out the window, Lane saw a newspaper delivery truck pull up near the restaurant. He was starting to feel uncomfortable. Claustrophobic. He had to get out.

He figured he might as well see what was in the news today.

"I'm gonna get a paper," he told Bob, and stood up. The waitress smiled as she watched Lane leave.

"Now, did I scare him off?" she asked Bob.

"You tell him I won't bite if he looks me in the eye next time."

Bob eased himself back into the cushions of the booth and fixed the waitress with his Cheshire-cat smile.

"Didn't your mamma ever tell you never to trust a man that can look a pretty woman in the eye?"

Bob held the waitress's look, his grin frozen in place, his eyes never faltering. She looked away, then hurried off.

Bob turned and looked out the window at Lane. He wasn't smiling anymore. He was thinking things over. Things about Lane's story. Some of those things made him kind of wonder.

Bob's thoughts were broken by the sound of a hacking cough that came from the counter just to his left.

Bob turned as the coughing grew louder and more frequent.

It was the trucker whom they'd overheard talking to the cook a few minutes ago. He was having some kind of spasm, some kind of attack. People all over the diner were beginning to look his way.

Bob stopped another waitress who was passing by.

"Hey, bring that guy some water," he told her. As she went off to get it, he called over to the trucker, "Hang in there, bud. Water's on the way."

Outside in the falling snow, Lane waited for the newspaper deliveryman to finish loading the coin-op dispensers.

"Anything interesting today?" he asked.

The guy answered him by handing him a paper and pointing to a front-page headline.

"Nuggets won," he said.

So directed, Lane didn't see what else was on the front page.

It also bore a photo of the Tall Indian Motel in Amarillo, where the grisly double murder had been discovered.

Instead Lane gave him thirty-five cents and flipped straight to the sports section.

The trucker's coughing was coming faster and louder. The glass of water the waitress had given the trucker hadn't helped a bit. In fact it had only seemed to make things worse.

The trucker was doubled over on his stool. His face had turned beet red. He'd dropped the glass, spilling water all over himself and the countertop.

Fighting for air, the trucker tried to get off the stool and struggle onto his feet. He managed to take only one step before he collapsed to the floor, gasping and choking like a fish stranded on dry land.

By now the waitress was screaming and the cook, who'd come out of the kitchen, was hollering. Bob was on his feet too. Kneeling beside the trucker, he could see he wasn't breathing anymore.

"Call an ambulance right away!" he yelled at the waitress who stood next to him. "This guy ain't breathing!"

Panic had made the waitress freeze up. She just stood there as a crowd began to gather.

The only one thinking straight seemed to be the cook, who came around the counter and tried to administer the Heimlich maneuver. But as he attempted to wrap his arms around the trucker's midsection, he found his girth too large to permit him to perform the lifesaving technique.

"Goddammit Fae!" the cook hollered at the waitress, looking up. "Call the ambulance!"

"He's gonna die!" the waitress yelled back. She worked her mouth just fine, but the rest of her was frozen in place. "Jesus, he's gonna die!"

One glance at the stricken truck driver told Bob that the waitress was right on the money on that call.

The poor bastard sure looked like a goner.

Lane came back into the restaurant and saw the crowd that had gathered near the counter. He spotted Bob amid the throng and could just make out that there was someone lying on the floor at the base of the stools.

Quickly crossing the restaurant, Lane flung his newspaper into his booth as he drew closer.

Now he was near enough to recognize the checkered mackinaw of the truck driver that had been sitting adjacent to them at the counter a few minutes before.

"Let me look at him," Lane shouted, elbowing his way into the crowd. "I'm a doctor!"

As the crowd parted for him, Lane knelt beside the stricken trucker. He immediately went to work, checking the sick man's vital signs.

Pulse, retinal reflexes, skin pallidity—all the signs were bad. The man was definitely fading fast.

The cook quickly explained what had happened.

From the description, it was clear to Lane that the trucker had sustained a severe tracheal blockage that was occluding his windpipe. He would certainly die unless whatever had caused the blockage was immediately removed.

This meant one of two things. Get him breathing fast in the hopes of dislodging the object or, failing that, perform an emergency tracheotomy.

Lane could afford to waste no time. He had

to act immediately in order to save the man's life.

"Get him on the counter," he told the cook, who with the help of Bob and a few other restaurant patrons lifted up the trucker and laid him across the top of the lunch counter, sending dishes of food and cups and glasses full of liquids crashing to the floor.

Tearing open the stricken man's shirt, Lane immediately began emergency CPR. Before doing anything else, he had to try getting his heart going again.

"Sweet Jesus!" wailed the waitress as Lane began pounding the area at the base of the trucker's heart in an attempt to shock the aortal muscle into action. "He's turning blue!"

"Get in the kitchen, Fae!" the cook shouted at the waitress. He didn't need Howard Cosell screaming in his ear at a time like this. "Go on, damn it!"

Lane hit the trucker's heart zone again and again, but each time he listened for a pulse the result was the same.

Nothing.

The stricken man was not responding. The clock was working against Lane, he realized. He could continue trying to get his heart going, but in that case his trachea would still be blocked and he could still die of suffocation.

Lane made a snap decision. He would go for the tracheotomy in the hopes that clearing his air tube would enable him to get the man breathing again.

Seeing the young waitress who'd tried to flirt with him before, Lane instructed her to bring him clean towels, a thick straw, one of the plastic ones that come with "go cups," boiling water, and some kind of disinfectant—rubbing alcohol, even whiskey if nothing else was available.

The waitress rushed into the kitchen, returning in seconds with towels. Then she set out for the straw.

The cook had already reached under the counter and produced a first-aid kit, throwing its contents across the counter as he rummaged around for the bottle of isopropyl alcohol he knew was in the kit. A second or two later, Lane was grasping both towels and alcohol from their hands.

Pulling a jackknife from his pocket, Lane flicked open the blade. Pouring some alcohol over the blade to sterilize it, he splashed the remainder of the small bottle over the tracheal region of the trucker's exposed throat.

Then he took the straw from the returning waitress, dousing it with alcohol also. The rest of it took place just as the medical textbooks dictated.

He made a one-centimeter incision in the region below the blockage and inserted the straw.

The results were nearly textbook-perfect too. Almost instantaneously the trucker's breathing reflexes took over and he began to inhale. Lane put his ear against his patient's heart region. The heart was now beating. Beating weakly but steadily. Lane knew that the man would live.

When he looked up again, Lane saw Bob watching him intently. Bob wasn't smiling anymore. He looked awestruck.

"Goddamn, boy!"

Bob and Lane stood outside in the restaurant's parking lot, watching amid the falling snow as a county emergency-services ambulance crew took the trucker out of the restaurant on a stretcher.

Bob grinned from ear to ear.

"Goddamn!" he repeated. "*Doctor* Dixon! I'd of never figured it."

He slapped Lane on the back for the twentieth time in the last five minutes. In his enthusiasm, Bob hadn't noticed that Lane wasn't even smiling.

"Don't call me that," he told him.

"What the hell do you mean, 'Don't call me that'?" Bob retorted. "I didn't make that up, son. You called yourself one."

"It clears a path," Lane said.

"Don't give me that bull-shit!" Bob said. "You don't think I was born yesterday, do ya, pardner? What you did back there wasn't something you learned in some damn book. You've had training."

Lane was silent, staring at Bob and holding his look but saying nothing.

Bob went on, "Now, maybe you been to med school and dropped out or maybe you been in the army. But don't tell me you ain't no doctor, 'cause by god I was just in the operating room with you."

"Look, I don't want to talk about it," Lane answered finally, his voice barely above an angry whisper.

Without another word, Lane climbed into the Caddy.

Bob went around to the driver's side, shaking his head.

He paused for a second or two to watch the ambulance drive off, its lights flashing, and then vanish around a turn in the highway.

"Goddamn! Doctor Dixon," he said once again, as he got in beside Lane.

9

The accordion folders atop the desk in Olmstead's office bulged with yellowed newspaper clippings. There were six of them in all, not counting the old satchel of chafed and weather-beaten leather that was also full of file material.

Taking out one of the folders, LaCrosse turned it on its belly and riffled through its contents for a minute. Then he pulled one of the clippings, spread it flat on the desk, and spun it around too, so Olmstead and Nate, who sat across from him, could look it over.

The newspaper item was dated some three years earlier.

The story concerned the death of a John Doe found in a field adjacent to a secondary road near Antler, Wyoming. The accompanying photograph depicted the murder victim's body, covered by a sheet and surrounded by sheriff's deputies.

"He started with the unconnected victim,"

LaCrosse narrated. "The runaway, the hitch-hiker, the wino. They're invisible when alive and forgotten when dead."

LaCrosse took another clipping from the folder and laid it beside the first one. The story concerned another murder, this one of a man whose face, sardonically set in a death rictus, was shown in the grainy black-and-white photograph.

"He's credited with at least eighteen known deaths," LaCrosse said to Olmstead and Nate. "There's no way of knowing how many came before he began telling us about them."

Olmstead looked up from the desk at LaCrosse. Nate did too. The sheriff and his deputy traded glances.

"He *tells* you about them?" Nate asked. "What's he do, call you?"

LaCrosse looked at Nate, then Olmstead.

"He writes," he said without a trace of a smile. "And he sends me these," he added, pulling two more clippings concerning the serial killer's past murders from another of the folders.

"Why you, Frank?" asked Olmstead.

"I headed a task force that tracked him for fifteen months," LaCrosse answered, tapping his finger on one of the two photos that accompanied the article, which was from the *Cleveland Plain Dealer.*

Olmstead looked to where LaCrosse was pointing.

The photo was of LaCrosse. Its caption stated that LaCrosse was charged with apprehending the killer and had been given special powers by the Department of Justice.

LaCrosse took out another group of clippings, which moved in chronological order from that point.

"After the task force was set up, he changed tactics. He got bolder," LaCrosse said. "Took more chances."

This was plain from the more grisly nature of the newer homicides, and their frequency. Now he was doing two or even three at a time.

"He saw the murders as a kind of competition," LaCrosse said. "He took his publicity seriously."

The headlines from some of the newer clippings underscored what LaCrosse was saying. KILLER TAUNTS INVESTIGATORS, one read. "But it became harder for him and we got closer." Another headline read: TASK FORCE CLOSING IN ON KILLER.

LaCrosse laid a final clipping on the table.

Its photo depicted the prone body of the murdered baby-sitter in a contorted death posture.

He stared at this photo awhile and rubbed his eyes as though they stung him. Finally he looked up. Olmstead and Nate were watching him carefully.

"Five months ago," LaCrosse told them. "He stopped."

"Why, Frank?" asked Olmstead.

"I don't know," he replied. "He's been quiet till now."

Olmstead had been a cop for a long time and knew that what LaCrosse was telling them was just the tip of the iceberg. There was a whole lot more lying beneath the surface that LaCrosse wasn't sharing with them, and he wanted to know what that was and why the Fed was holding it back.

Before Olmstead could say anything else, though, LaCrosse's wristwatch beeped.

"I need to make a call," he said, turning it off.

"Go on into my office, Frank, and use the phone."

Olmstead waited until LaCrosse was gone a solid minute before he studied the final clipping.

"Maybe he's onto something, maybe not," he told Nate. "But one thing's certain—he knows this killer."

Nate, who was studying another of the clippings, shook his head. Something was bothering the deputy.

"What're you thinking, Nate?"

"I'm thinking that it's eight A.M.," he said,

laying down the sheet of faded yellow news-print again, "the polls are open, and I just hope to God we're hunting the right guy."

Alone in Olmstead's office, LaCrosse sat on the edge of the sheriff's sofa and chucked the receiver between his shoulder and his chin.

"It's me," he said.

"Amarillo," he continued. He nodded as he spoke into the mouthpiece. "Since about four this morning. No, I was too late again."

He sat up a bit as he listened. "They did? When? What did you tell them?"

Then he shook his head.

"No, don't cry, honey. I don't think they know I'm here yet."

He paused again, listening, briefly closing his eyes.

"I'll deal with that when it comes. Love you."

LaCrosse slowly racked the handset.

As he did, he noticed the awards, plaques, photographs, and newspaper clippings on the wall. One award was for bravery under fire.

LaCrosse touched one and studied it for a minute. Then he turned and walked back out the door.

The white Eldorado took the tortuous switchbacking turns of the high mountain road with the surefooted grace of a mountain gazelle.

Even in the heavy snow that now fell across the Sangre de Cristo, its tires gripped the slick road surface.

Bob, behind the wheel, whistled softly to himself. He knew every inch of these roads, and had taken them in foul weather and fair. It would be a cakewalk.

"You're a strange one, Doc," he said, turning to Lane, who no longer bothered telling him to stop calling him that, since Goodall obviously was not about to listen to him. "Smart. Cool under pressure. Yet something's digging into you just like a rusty pair of spurs."

Lane ignored him and pointedly stared out the window at the falling snow that was blanketing the high mountain passes.

"Okay," Bob said with resignation after awhile. "You don't want to talk about it, that's your business, but—"

"I quit," Lane cut in, turning from the window to Bob. He had a strange look on his face. "I was in the first three months of my surgery residency," he said. "I was good. Hell, I was cocky, I thought I was so good."

He shook his head, laughed.

"I used to watch other post-graduates wash out and think, that'll never happen to me. Well, here I am."

"What happened? You have a patient die on

you or something?" Bob wanted to know.

"Yeah."

"Hell. That's gonna happen. But you go home, get some sleep, and next day you try again. That's life."

"I tried that route," Lane answered. "But the next day it was worse. And the day after . . ." Lane watched Bob nod and went on, "The psychiatrists at school said I was going through what they called 'a crisis of confidence.' Nothing a little rest couldn't fix."

"Well, you sure seemed cured today," Bob countered.

"This time, yeah," Lane said. "But what about the next time?"

"What do you want, guarantees?" Bob scolded. "Man, there ain't no guarantees. 'Specially out here."

Bob gestured through the windshield at the stony granite flanks of the surrounding mountains.

"Out here folks know this. They know that risk's a part of life, and they ain't looking for some equalizer to change the rules of the game."

Bob fell silent. He was getting mad.

He hit the steering wheel with the heel of his hand, pulled onto the shoulder, and turned off the windshield wipers.

Snow covered the glass as fast as if somebody had flung a white blanket over the car, but still Bob looked straight ahead, not wanting to turn his head at Lane.

"What a waste," he said under his breath. "What a goddamn waste."

Lane was silent for a long beat. Finally he too spoke up.

"Yeah, I've heard that before," he told Bob.

"I bet you have," Bob answered him, finally looking him in the face. "But unlike anyone else in your life, *I've* got nothing invested in you. All *I* know is what I saw back there—a man dying and a roomful of people who would have given their right arms to save him."

Bob's voice rose and his face hardened as he went on, "*You* had the power and you didn't hesitate. And that man will go home to his wife, maybe his children, because of you."

Bob fell silent but Lane didn't reply. Bob turned back to the windshield. "My father used to say to my brother and me, 'Nerve succeeds,'" Bob went on. "You got the nerve, Doc. I've seen it up close. If you really were a quitter, you'd have stood around like the rest of us."

Bob hit the wiper button and in three fast sweeps the windshield was clear. He put the Caddy back in drive and swung it back onto the road.

10

A babble of voices, punctuated now and then by the ringing of phones and the squawking of police radios, filled the conference room of the Amarillo Sheriff's Department building, where a command post had been set up.

Its walls were covered with large, detailed maps of the region. Bunches of colored pushpins indicated sites where the killer had struck. Uniformed deputies periodically went from the phones to the maps, adding new pins or moving existing ones around.

Trestle tables supporting computers, telephones, TV screens, fax machines, printers, and stacks of files occupied the center of the large enclosure. At one of these, Frank La-Crosse, Nate, and two other deputies analyzed breaking information pertinent to the case. Olmstead looked on, sipping from a mug of coffee.

"As of seven-thirty this morning, we have six reported missing persons," one of the deputies said, reading from a computer printout. "Three of those are women. Five are homeless men who didn't report to shelters last night."

"Rule out the homeless," LaCrosse told him as Olmstead's secretary, Becky, came in and walked over to where Olmstead stood observing things and sipping his coffee. "He needed transportation."

"Sheriff, Mr. Saldez's attorney, Mr. Martinez, is here," she broke in. "He's breathing fire about Mr. LaCrosse shooting his client."

Olmstead thanked her. He turned to LaCrosse.

"We need him to cooperate, Frank. Maybe Nate and I should talk to him alone."

"No. I'll talk to him," LaCrosse replied.

"Fine." Buck headed for his office, where the suspect's attorney waited. Nate and LaCrosse followed, only to be stopped as a deputy came up and spoke to LaCrosse.

"Preliminary lab results just came back about the hair they found in the bed," he told the FBI man. "Definitely not Saldez's." He handed LaCrosse a computer printout showing the lab results.

"A 36052," LaCrosse said, half to himself as he scanned the printout.

"A what?" the deputy asked.

LaCrosse pocketed the printout. He merely smiled at the deputy as he walked out into the hall.

*   *   *

Jorge Martinez was a man not accustomed to taking shit from anyone, especially the police, whom he dealt with regularly in his role as a court-appointed criminal defense lawyer. Behind Martinez's back, they called him "The Pit Bull."

This had as much to do with his manner as with his appearance. Martinez was a short, tanklike man, who wore his hair closely cropped in an almost military-like crew cut, and who carried himself with the belligerence of a bantam rooster.

Olmstead and Nate had already exchanged pleasantries with the Pit Bull. But LaCrosse was on top of Martinez's hit list for the day. As soon as LaCrosse walked in, Martinez went on the attack.

"Special Agent Frank LaCrosse," he said, forcing a tactical smile. "Am I glad to see you."

"Thank you for coming in, Mr. Martinez." LaCrosse welcomed him, unaware whom he was dealing with.

"Oh, I wouldn't miss it," the Pit Bull countered, stroking the corner of his mustache. "I wanted to thank you personally for making my job of defending Hector Saldez so easy."

"And how's that?" LaCrosse asked, sensing he was being set up for something but not yet realizing what.

"How's that?" Martinez countered immediately, knowing the prey had just fallen into his trap.

His voice rose an octave and he began to pace the room, waving his hands as he spoke.

"How's about violating three of my client's constitutional rights for openers?"

The Pit Bull spun on his heels and pointed his finger at LaCrosse.

Martinez was just getting warmed up.

"How's torturing him?" he shouted even louder. "How's illegally questioning him? How's failure to advise him of his rights."

The Pit Bull composed himself and again resumed his tactical smile as he crossed his arms and rocked on his heels, Mussolini-style. "Like I said before, *thank you*, Mr. LaCrosse. You're a godsend."

"May I remind you that your client was holding a knife on an innocent man," Olmstead put in before the Pit Bull revved himself up for another attack, hoping to slow him down some. The Sheriff had seen Martinez at work before.

"You can remind me all you want, Sheriff," Martinez told him. "It won't mean jack to a jury."

"So I take it you don't wish to cooperate with us about locating the car your client stole?" LaCrosse asked him.

Martinez turned back to LaCrosse and

flashed him a look reserved for children and submental idiots.

His smile got bigger and toothier. "Are you kidding or what?" he said. "I just came in here to thank you personally on behalf of my client, whom, by the way, I will also be representing in civil proceedings against you and the city. Good day, gentlemen."

Having delivered his master stroke, the Pit Bull picked up his briefcase and moved toward the doorway.

But just as he was about to stride through it, LaCrosse spoke up.

"Sit down, Mr. Martinez."

The Pit Bull froze in place. He slowly turned and glared at LaCrosse.

"Maybe you didn't hear me, my friend," he said. "I'm not staying."

"Yes, you are," LaCrosse said calmly.

In a flash the Pit Bull was back on the attack again.

"Oh, I'll stay, will I?" Martinez retorted. "And how do you propose to make me, Special Agent? Put a bullet in me too?"

LaCrosse's lips tightened in something resembling a smile as he reached into his pocket.

The Pit Bull's own smile drooped.

For a split second he thought the son-of-a-bitch was actually going to pull a gun on him.

But then the hand came out clutching a folded sheet of paper. It was the printout the deputy had given him awhile ago in the command post.

Before LaCrosse could say anything, though, the same deputy had come into the conference room. "The lab reports are just back," he told LaCrosse, who watched him with interest. "It's confirmed. Definitely a 36052."

For the first time since the Pit Bull had seen him, LaCrosse's smile was more than a simple tightening of the lips. A real smile now played across the special agent's face. LaCrosse thanked the deputy and turned to the Pit Bull.

"Well, Mr. Martinez," he said. "I'm sorry to have wasted your time. You can go." LaCrosse himself now got up to leave.

The Pit Bull stood there looking thunderstruck.

"Wait a minute," he protested. "What the hell's a . . . a three-six-oh-whatever?"

"It's just a lab term," LaCrosse answered. "A hair that we've found in the motel room." The FBI man was almost at the door. "We'll see you in court, Mr. Martinez."

"Lab term?" He put out an arm to stop LaCrosse before he left. Something was up. The Pit Bull could sense it. "Look, look," he said, now trying to cut a deal. "You wanted to know about the car, right?"

"It's not necessary now," LaCrosse said, and sidestepped the lawyer.

Martinez was experienced enough to know that things had changed drastically in the last few minutes. He wasn't about to be put off. "Look," he said. "I could tell you. If we made a deal."

"What kind of deal?" asked Buck.

"Drop the murder charges and I'll tell you where my client boosted the Explorer."

"Forget it," LaCrosse said, stepping completely through the door.

"You know you can't prove anything," the Pit Bull told him as he walked into the hall. "Not a single damn thing!"

"We'll see," LaCrosse said, and started down the hall as Martinez watched his back.

Olmstead was on his way out too. "Sorry," he told the Pit Bull as he passed the lawyer. "Sometimes you win and sometimes you lose." Nate said nothing as he left behind Olmstead.

At the last minute, the Pit Bull stepped into the hall.

"He boosted the car at the airport," he shouted after them.

LaCrosse stopped in place.

"Long-term parking. Lot C," Martinez went on.

LaCrosse looked at the lawyer.

"Thank you, Mr. Martinez," he said, and started to turn again.

"Hey, what about the hair?" the Pit Bull called out.

"Male, early twenties, brown hair," LaCrosse said over his shoulder, and kept walking.

The Pit Bull shook his head in disbelief. "Son of a bitch," he grumbled, knowing he'd been fooled—and embarrassed.

So that bastard Saldez didn't do the stiff in the car after all.

He made a promise to make sure Saldez knew how he'd had to kick ass all over the sheriff's office to find that out when he saw his client later that day.

But first some lunch. And maybe a couple of martinis. Dry, and only with the best Russian vodka.

"Go back to the waitresses at the restaurant," Olmstead told Bud, "and see if the hair color sparks anything."

They were back at the command center where Nate was already on the phone with airport security. With the announcement of the lab results, the cops assigned to the case got a major-league boost.

Olmstead turned to LaCrosse and smiled at the Fed as Bud left. "They teach you that little 36052 business back at the academy, Frank?" he asked.

"No, my wife did," LaCrosse said.

"What is she, a con-woman?"

"Sort of. She's a lawyer," LaCrosse answered.

Nate hung up the phone and turned to them both. "Airport security has video on all car license tags coming and going from their lots. We're pulling the last twenty-four hours and will cross-check it with stolen vehicles."

"Looks like you might have caught your first big break, Frank," Olmstead said to LaCrosse.

"Maybe," he said guardedly.

Nate looked at the clock. It was already ten A.M. "I think we ought to make an announcement, Buck," he told the sheriff, thinking about the election and that the news of the new lead might help give Olmstead an edge over McGinnis at the polls.

"We don't have anything yet," LaCrosse put in.

"Like hell we don't," Nate answered. "We know it's not Saldez for one thing. With that we can blow McGinnis's case right out of the water."

"You do that and you'd be telling the real killer we're on to him," LaCrosse countered.

Nate thought about this and then turned to Olmstead.

"I think we're missing a big opportunity here, Buck," he said. "Most folks in town are going to vote on their lunch hour. We've still got time."

"Is that all that's going on here?" LaCrosse put in. "Winning your goddamn election."

"That 'goddamn election' is my livelihood," Nate shot back at the Fed. "Now I realize that don't mean jack-shit to you. But I've worked my butt off in this office for fifteen years, and if Jack McGinnis wins, Buck won't be the only one to lose around here."

LaCrosse's glance fell on the deputies around him. He realized a dozen pairs of eyes were on him. He could tell which way they would vote on releasing the new evidence. But it was Olmstead's call to make.

"Only reason McGinnis hasn't made an announcement is because he doesn't have enough to charge Saldez," said the sheriff. "Until that time we'll sit pat too." He turned to Nate. "Find the car."

Becky stuck her head in the door. "Sheriff. Telephone."

Olmstead left the room to take the call. LaCrosse sat down at one of the tables, not wanting to meet anybody's glance.

Olmstead looked up from his desk as he punched the flashing button on the telephone and picked up the receiver. Nate had followed him into the office and stood by the desk.

"Olmstead here," he said into the mouth-piece.

The other end of the line connected to the FBI field office in Dallas, where a button-down guy in suspenders paced the office, talking at the speakerphone on his desk.

"Sheriff. Grant Montgomery, Internal Affairs, FBI," the crisp voice in Olmstead's ear said. "I understand Frank LaCrosse is in your custody."

"He's here. But not in our custody," Olmstead replied.

"The field office here in Dallas has been notified and a couple of agents should arrive within the next hour to take him off your hands," Montgomery said as though he hadn't heard a word Olmstead'd just uttered.

"Hold on there, Mr. Montgomery," Olmstead pushed. "He's working on a case here."

"He shouldn't be," Montgomery answered. "He should be in Philadelphia right now on another assignment, which he left twenty-four hours ago without authorization. And this isn't the first time, Sheriff. He's left posts three times in the last two months. He's currently on Bureau suspension."

"You going to tell me what he did wrong?"

"It's not your problem, Sheriff," Montgomery told him. "We'd appreciate it, however, if you'd hold him till our people arrive."

"What about your ongoing investigation

with this killer?" Olmstead asked as what Montgomery was saying to him began sinking in.

"There's no ongoing FBI investigation," Montgomery answered. "The case has been closed for five months."

"That's impossible," Olmstead protested, not knowing what else to say.

"Look, Sheriff," Montgomery began.

"No, *you* look," Olmstead shot back. "I've got three people dead in this town, and this man you're coming to pick up is the only damn person who seems to know what the hell is going on. . . ." Olmstead paused. "Now, I want some answers."

"I don't give a tin shit what you want, Sherriff," said Montgomery. "Right now the only thing you'd better deal with is keeping that man in sight until my people arrive. If that's too much to ask, I can have a U.S. marshal in your office in five minutes who *can* handle that kind of responsibility."

Now it was Montgomery's turn to pause.

"Are we clear, Sheriff? *One* hour."

Olmstead didn't say anything. There was nothing left to say.

He let the handset slip from his fingers back into its cradle and looked up at Nate.

"What the hell's going on?" Nate asked.

"I don't know," is all Olmstead could say, and he shook his head.

11

It was getting harder to see the road. On what he supposed was the margin, Lane winced as the edge of a snowflake got past his lashes and melted on his eyeball.

Lane turned back to the Caddy, parked a few feet away, at which Goodall was doing something under the hood.

About an hour ago, just after they'd begun climbing the pass into the mountains, the Caddy had begun to miss and finally stalled.

Bob had pulled the car over and gotten out to see what was the matter.

It was sure taking a long time, though.

Lane was beginning to shiver.

"Damn!" he heard Bob curse.

"What's wrong?" Lane asked. From his position he couldn't see Bob straining to loosen the frozen wing-nut that secured the cover of the air scoop, which sat just above the carburetor.

Bob didn't answer right away, he was too

intent on unthreading the nut that had finally come loose and removing the air scoop's cover to look inside.

"There it is," Bob said to himself. Just as he'd figured.

The two shutterlike flaps of the butterfly valve—which permitted oxygen to flow from the scoop into the carb, with gasoline, and be fired by the spark plugs—were closed. No air getting to the carb meant the engine would miss and finally stall out.

"It's like I thought," he finally answered Lane. "The car's not tuned for this elevation."

Bob was already getting out the ballpoint pen he'd stored in the glove compartment against just such an eventuality. Forcing open the butterfly valve, he inserted the pen between the flaps to keep them open.

"Did you fix it?" Lane asked as Bob went around and opened the driver's side door.

"Nope. Just patched it some till we get to the next town."

Bob turned the key in the ignition and the engine fired right up. Bob revved it a little then got back out again to look under the hood.

Everything was running smooth. He could hear the cylinders hitting perfectly now. He took the ballpoint back out and replaced the air-scoop cover. The valve would probably stay open for a while.

"Where's the next town?" Lane wanted to know as he watched Bob wipe his hands on a rag.

Bob slammed the hood and flashed Lane a smile.

"Not far."

The cold stung LaCrosse again. He held his hands under the stream of tapwater and splashed his face another time.

Better, he thought. That felt much better.

Closing the taps, LaCrosse wiped his face on a soft bathroom towel and stepped into the hallway of Buck Olmstead's house.

He'd noticed the framed family photographs that lined the walls on his way in and now stopped to look at them.

One in particular caught his eye.

The color print showed a much younger Olmstead and a strikingly beautiful woman next to each other on horseback.

LaCrosse went down the hall and into the kitchen, where Olmstead stood at the sink slicing tomatoes. Bacon was already sizzling atop the stove.

"Is that your wife?" he asked.

"Yep, Frank. That sure is," Olmstead answered.

"Beautiful woman."

"Thank you, Frank," Olmstead said, his words punctuated by the tapping of the knife edge as it hit the cutting board. "We were married thirty-two years ago. Been two years since she passed away."

"I'm sorry," LaCrosse said.

Olmstead reached over to turn down the heat under the bacon, saying, "She was a wonderful woman," as he went back to his slicing.

"Where'd you meet your wife, Frank?" Olmstead asked.

"In law school."

"So you're a lawyer too?"

"I never took the bar," LaCrosse replied. "I did a fieldwork internship with the Bureau one summer and never looked back."

"Children?"

"One," LaCrosse said.

"What's your wife think about you traipsing all over the country?" Olmstead asked, setting up a plate lined with paper towels.

"Actually, she's very understanding."

Olmstead glanced over at the bacon. Judging it crisp enough, he turned off the heat, then laid the strips on the towels to absorb the fat.

"That's key," he told LaCrosse, getting out two more plates, a jar of mustard, and a bottle of ketchup. "Hungry? Sit yourself down. Food'll be ready in a second."

Olmstead set the two plates and the condiments on the table and went back to the countertop, where the bacon was draining, the lettuce and tomatoes sat in the colander, and the fresh loaf of whole wheat bread waited to be opened.

LaCrosse stood by the chair but did not sit down.

"No thanks," he said.

"Nonsense," Olmstead said, putting the bacon on the bread. "I make the very best BLTs in this part of the country. Secret's in the tomatoes. Grow my own in a greenhouse all winter, and—"

"He took my son."

Olmstead stopped making the sandwiches and turned around.

"You asked me why he stopped killing," LaCrosse said. "We were getting close. We'd had several breaks. Outside of Boston we had roadblocks up within twenty minutes of a murder there. He slipped through. Everyone felt it was just a matter of time before we nailed him."

LaCrosse stopped for a moment to collect his thoughts. "By taking my son—"

"He got you removed from the case."

LaCrosse nodded.

"The kidnapping had the highest priority, even though the Bureau never received a note or demands. And almost immediately, they found new clues. They closed in on a man in Wisconsin."

LaCrosse reached into the pocket of his

jacket, produced a yellowed newspaper clipping, and handed it to Olmstead. It was one the sheriff had never seen before. The grainy photo showed a body hanging from a noose.

"When they caught up with him, they found him strung up in his motel room," LaCrosse explained. "Suicide. He'd left detailed notes about the victims, things only the killer would know. As well as this."

Now LaCrosse handed Olmstead a glossy color photo.

It showed a little boy sitting in a chair in a hallway, clutching a patchwork quilt to his chest. Behind him a shaft of sunlight cut across the hall, providing just enough light to show the boy had been crying.

Frank motioned for Buck to turn the photo over.

Buck read the scrawl he found there: "Two-eighteen. To find him you must kill me. To understand me, you must come to *believe*."

"Two-eighteen?" Olmstead asked, flipping the photo back over. "What's that mean?"

"I don't know," LaCrosse said. "Eighteen victims? Eighteenth of February? It could mean anything."

"Eighteenth of February's the day after tomorrow," Olmstead ventured aloud, but the thought didn't take him anywhere. "So what happened to the investigation?"

"After a month and a half they closed the case."

"But you don't think he's dead."

"It was too easy," LaCrosse said. "But when I tried convincing somebody of that, they shot me down."

"You were just the heartsick father unable to let go of the hope," Olmstead returned.

LaCrosse nodded. "Then about a month ago, I heard about a murder. The way the victim was killed. I knew immediately it was him. I've been following him since."

Olmstead handed back the photo.

"And your son?" he asked LaCrosse. "Do you still think he's alive."

LaCrosse put the photo away again.

He did not look at it as he slid it into his pocket.

"I don't have any choice," he said.

12

"Texas plate," Bud said to Nate, his eyes on the playback of the airport security video.

For hours the deputies had been watching footage of vehicles entering and leaving the Amarillo Airport's parking facilities, their eyes straining to discern the numerals on hundreds of license tags.

Bud fed the latest sequence of tag numbers into the computer terminal in front of him.

234-453.

He didn't expect anything; none of the other entries had come up aces. He even miskeyed a stroke at first, he'd grown so tired of the painstaking work.

But seconds later, after the state Motor Vehicles Department's database had been accessed, the picture suddenly changed.

"Wait a minute," Nate said, rechecking the plate number. He hardly believed what he was seeing.

He began reading the data off the monitor.

"James Ruskin. Missing from Midland, two days ago. Last seen driving a 1977 Cadillac Eldorado. White."

Nate turned to Bud.

"Tell Becky to get the word out."

The mechanic's name was Shorty. At least that's what he'd told Lane.

Anyway, he looked like a guy you'd call Shorty, Lane thought as he sat on a metal-topped stool, sipping hot coffee and watching the mechanic tighten a nut on the Caddy's undercarriage.

Shorty had the car up on a pneumatic lift. He'd been at it for about half an hour, more or less.

Bob had headed straight for the garage as soon as they'd reached the town, which was somewhere in Colorado and called Martinsburg. At least Lane thought it was Colorado. Maybe New Mexico. He'd have to ask Bob about that.

For now, though, he was content to be in a warm place out of the snow, watching Shorty work on the car and listening to the country and western stuff that was playing on the garage's radio.

"That fella and me went to school together, went to work together," Shorty was telling Lane as he finished up, meaning Bob, who was off wandering around the garage. He lowered the car back down again. "He was the best man at my wedding."

Opening the hood, Shorty picked up a torque wrench and started working on the engine.

"Broke my back two years ago," he went on to Lane. "Want to guess who fed my kids while I was laid up?"

As if Lane couldn't, Shorty pointed the wrench at Bob, who was now stroking his chin contemplatively in front of a battle-scarred candy machine that dated back to 1954. "Paid my bills. Every last one of 'em till I could get back to work."

"Come on, Shorty," Bob called back, feeding the machine some change. "You're making me sound like a saint."

Nothing happened, and Bob took to jabbing the coin-return button. When this didn't work either he took to slamming the side of the machine with the palm of his hand.

"That's broken, Bob," Shorty told him. "Gonna have to remember to get it fixed."

Bob took to wandering the garage again, disappearing into Shorty's cramped and messy office.

"What kind of work did you and Bob do?" Lane asked the mechanic.

"We cleared passes for the Rio Grande," he answered. "A storm like this'll drop a foot and a half, maybe two feet up there in those passes. Somebody's got to clear 'em to get the freight through. That was our job."

"When did you start doing this?"

"When I got back from 'Nam," he answered. "Got married and had me a family. Figured if I made it through Tet, I wasn't gonna tempt fate much more bein' up there in those chutes on a night like tonight."

Just then the hourly news came on the country-western station on the radio. The announcer was talking about the murders in Amarillo.

"Hey, Bob," Shorty called out to Goodall, who was in his office where the radio was, "turn that up."

Bob did, and the announcer's amplified voice continued. "... Amarillo City Police have confirmed they have a suspect in custody in connection with the shooting in a local apartment complex early this morning, but as yet the suspect has not been charged in connection with the two brutal murders at a local motel. . . ."

The news shifted to another topic and Shorty shook his head.

"Bad business," he said, turning to Lane. "Last two day's I been carrying around this little number."

Lifting his vest he showed Lane the butt of a pistol holstered at his hip.

Bob returned to the bay. "Better be careful with that."

"Can't be too careful's what I say," Shorty said, covering up the gun again.

Bob grabbed his coat and hat. He made to head for the door.

"You going somewhere?" Lane asked him.

"Wanna stretch my legs," he said, then to Shorty, "How long before we're ready to go here?"

"Ten minutes," Shorty replied. "But you ain't going nowhere. You're staying with us tonight."

Bob was already half out the door.

"Next time," he said.

Before Shorty could argue, he was gone.

Through swirling flakes of snow, Bob looked across the deserted street. He could barely make out the red-lettered sign of a combination grocery and hardware store on the opposite side. Turning up his collar, Bob headed for the store.

"Sweet tooth," Shorty told Lane with a chuckle as they watched Bob through a window fronting the street.

"What?" Lane asked.

"He wouldn't tell you, but Bob's got himself a mighty vicious sweet tooth."

Inside the store, Bob looked around. Except for the young woman at the checkout counter, the place looked completely deserted.

He went over to her, his eyes flicking across

her face. Pretty. Then down to her name tag. Betty.

He figured Betty for about twenty-five. Bob flashed her one of his toothy smiles and waved his hand at the window.

"Pretty when it comes down like that." He didn't take his eyes off her.

"If it gets any prettier," she sullenly answered, glancing outside, "I'll be spending the night here tonight."

Bob grinned and pointed to the candy island in the center of the store. "I wanted to get some candy," he told her.

The checkout girl walked back to the island. Bob followed her, his eyes sweeping the store. Some old tinsel remained on display at the end of one empty aisle. Not a creature was stirring, Bob thought.

"Pretty quiet," he offered.

"Quiet isn't the word," Betty told him. "I broke my tail to get into work today, nearly ran off the road twice." She sounded exasperated. "Now I'm the only one here."

"What about your boss?"

"He calls in and says *he* can't get in," she replied. "I told him there wasn't a living soul here in town. But does he tell me to close and try to make it home before I get stuck?" she continued. "Hell, no. I'm supposed to keep the place open till one."

Betty gestured to the drifts piling up outside. "Now look at it. I'll be lucky to find my car, let alone get out." She went back to the subject at hand. "What'll you have?" she asked Bob.

"Candy corn. Small bag," he said.

Betty nodded and began filling a bag with a small plastic scoop. She liked candy corn too.

"Why don't you just lock up the store and not tell him?" Bob asked her, watching her work. Such small hands.

"I would, but he's going to call and check. Otherwise, believe me, I'd be out of here." She put the bag on a digital scale. "Hey, listen," she said to Bob, handing him the bag. "I didn't mean to bend your ear with this. It's two dollars, seventy-five cents."

Bob pulled a roll of bills from his pocket and peeled off a five. Betty watched him, thinking it was a pretty fat bankroll. Bob started handing her the five when the phone in the back room began to warble.

"That's him," Betty said, and darted to the back of the store without taking Bob's money.

Bob shrugged, listening to the phone conversation in the otherwise silent store, then put the money away.

As Betty spoke on the phone, he slowly crossed to the front door and looked out. Snow was piling up higher and higher by the minute, and plenty more of it was still coming down. Nothing moved on the deserted street except the wind.

Bob opened up the crinkly white bag Betty had just given him. Popping a handful of candy corn into his mouth, he reached out and nonchalantly turned the Come In, We're Open sign around so that it now read Closed to the street.

He swallowed his mouthful and smiled.

Sure was good candy corn.

He turned and walked back into the store.

Shorty dropped the Caddy's hood and wiped his hands on an oily rag.

"That's it," he told Lane. "Better tell Bob."

As Lane was putting on his coat, a car pulled up to the pumps outside the station. Its flanks were emblazoned with the shield of the Colorado Highway Patrol.

Lane watched the state trooper come in through the garage door, stamping twice to shake off the snow on his boots.

"Hey, Shorty, how about some gas," the trooper said.

"Comin' up. You finished for the day, John?" Shorty replied.

"Hell no," the trooper answered. "Just startin'."

The trooper noticed the Caddy as Lane started for the garage door. "She's sure a beaut," he remarked. "That yours?"

"No," Lane returned. "A friend of mine's." The trooper nodded and Lane left the garage.

"Nice paint job," the trooper said to Shorty after Lane had gone.

"Wait'll you see the interior," Shorty told him.

Shorty stood watching with an impish grin on his face as the trooper got his first look at the inside of Bob's vehicle. Just as Shorty'd figured, the trooper did an instant double-take. Then he leaned in and took a long second look.

Betty was still on the phone.

"That's right, Larry," she said to the party on the other end of the line. "Not a soul the whole morning. I wish you were paying me what you're spending to heat the place."

Betty glanced up to see Bob standing in the doorway, holding up the fiver with which he'd tried to pay for the candy corn.

Betty quickly held her index finger to her lips.

She wanted him to be quiet.

Bob nodded, understanding. Nobody was supposed to be in the store. He'd play along.

As he looked around the back room, Bob noticed a long worktable on which lay a couple of rolls of strapping tape and a box cutter. He picked up the letter and slowly slid the blade in and out.

Bob's eyes flicked back to Betty.

She was looking at him as she talked to her boss. Bob smiled at her, then glanced back around the room as Betty continued speaking.

"Thanks, Larry," she said to her boss. "You're doing the right thing. Yeah, I promise. I'll see you tomorrow. Bye."

Betty hung up, her relief obvious on her face. Bob held up the five dollar bill again.

"You didn't take my money," he said, stepping closer to her.

"Oh, forget it," she told him. "If I rang it up, he'd see it tomorrow and give me hell."

"Well, at least let me buy you a cup of coffee."

Betty flashed Bob a smile but didn't answer right away as she went over to her locker.

"Thanks," she said over her shoulder, "but I better hit the road while I got the chance."

Bob watched her take her purse from the locker. He stepped closer as she was occupied with her things, passing the worktable between the locker area and the door.

"I hate to ask," she said, still taking things from the locker, "but I know I'm gonna need a hand getting my car out."

She turned suddenly and saw that Bob stood almost directly behind her. She looked surprised, though not alarmed. "Then, maybe we could . . ." she began, her voice trailing off.

"Maybe? You wouldn't lead me on, would

you?" Bob asked her, looking into her eyes.

Betty looked back at him, holding his glance.

Suddenly somebody called Bob's name. Bob snapped around and took a step toward the front.

"Shit," Betty cursed. "Somebody's here," and she brushed past Bob into the store.

Bob followed her at a distance.

Lane was standing by the door.

Bob noticed he was holding a new cowboy hat. Probably bought it at the place just down the street, he figured. Wouldn't be surprised if the Doc bought a set of chaps next. After what had happened in the diner, nothing about Lane would surprise him anymore.

"Shorty's finished with the car," Lane called out to him.

"Thanks."

Turning to Betty, Bob tipped his hat.

"Sorry I can't help you," he told her, "but I gotta hit the road myself right about now."

Betty smiled and Bob stepped outside, Lane right behind him. Then he noticed the Closed sign.

Still holding the door open, Lane flipped it back over.

"The wind must have turned it around," he told Betty, and followed Bob along the snow-covered sidewalk.

Betty stood regarding the sign for a minute.

The wind had never done that before.

She locked the door and watched both men trudge across the street through the drifts.

Turning to go back to her locker, she noticed a box cutter lying on one of the checkout counters. What was that doing there? It looked like the one they usually kept in the stockroom.

Betty picked up the knife and stared at it, then looked out the plate-glass door at Bob's back.

Finally she picked up the box cutter and took it with her. Had to just be her imagination, she thought as she went over to her locker.

Outside, Lane and Bob were picking their way across the snowbound street.

"Sorry if I interrupted something back there," Lane told his friend.

"You flatter me, Doc," Bob told him. "Nice hat, by the way."

Suddenly Bob froze in midstep.

Through the dense snowfall, Bob had spotted the Colorado Highway Patrol vehicle parked outside Shorty's garage.

Bob said nothing and simply watched as the trooper came out a beat later, shook hands with Shorty, climbed in, and drove off.

Then he started walking again.

*   *   *

The garage door was open and Lane was backing the Eldorado out of the service bay into the snow.

"I wish you fellas would change your minds," Shorty told Bob as they both stood outside the place.

"Next time, Shorty."

Bob embraced his old friend as Lane aimed the car up the street, then climbed into the shotgun seat.

Shorty went back inside the garage and began pulling the bay door closed. As Lane turned the wheel to get the Caddy into the street, Bob stared at the door.

"Hey, stop," he suddenly said. "I forgot something. Be right back." He was already cracking the passenger side door and climbing out to slip beneath the garage door before it came to.

Inside, Bob heard the sound of running water. It came from the bathrooms off the office.

"Shorty?" he called out.

"Yo, Bob!" came Shorty's voice, echoing out of the bathroom. "Forget something?"

Bending slightly forward, Bob reached under the cuff of his jeans and pulled something loose with a faint rustle.

"Yeah, it's me," he called back to his old buddy from 'Nam.

As he walked back toward the office, the eight-inch blade of a knife gleamed in his hand, its cold malevolence mirrored by the icy expression that came over Bob's face.

As Bob stepped into the office he spotted Shorty by the sink, washing his hands, his back turned toward him.

"If you're gonna try to force money on me, you know better," Shorty called over his shoulder as he reached for a towel and dried his face, " 'cause I ain't accepting a penny."

When Shorty lowered the towel again, Bob was standing in front of him, eyes hard and cruel.

"What's wrong, buddy?" Shorty asked.

Bob answered with a single step closer, which plunged the blade, held down, deep into Shorty.

Bob cracked the Caddy's door and climbed back inside.

"Okay, let's roll," he told Lane with a smile.

Lane chanced to look down and saw the cuff of Bob's right pant leg caught over the top of his cowboy boot.

The handle of a knife was jutting out, and Lane's eyes lingered on it. Following Lane's glance, Bob noticed what he'd been staring at and reached down to free the cuff. Lane looked at Bob but didn't put the car into gear yet.

"Did he accept it?" he asked.

"Huh?"

"The money," Lane explained. "You tried to pay him, didn't you? Shorty told me he'd never take a cent from you."

Grinning, Lane put the Eldorado into drive. Bob smiled back at him. "This time I made him."

The Caddy pulled away from the garage and was quickly lost in the blizzard.

13

Nate was in Becky's office talking about nothing special when the fax started spitting paper. Nate pulled the sheet as it came off the machine and read it.

His jaw suddenly dropped.

"Get Buck," he told her.

As Becky went to phone the sheriff, neither of them were aware that two men in dark suits were flashing FBI shields at the receptionist, who pointed them down the hall toward Olmstead's office.

"When did he spot it?"

Olmstead was on the phone in his kitchen. He was talking to Nate back at the Amarillo Sheriff's Department.

"Twenty minutes ago at a gas station in Martinsburg," Nate told him, reading off the fax. "He didn't know it was hot. The trooper's going back to investigate."

Olmstead nodded at LaCrosse, who stood

by him and knew what the conversation must involve.

"Did he get a description of the driver?" Olmstead wanted to know.

"White male," Nate replied. "Late twenties. Blond to light brown hair."

Nate looked at a black-and-white photo on Olmstead's desk. The shot had been pulled from the raw video feed of the restaurant's security-tape footage. It showed the rancher, his daughter, and Lane Dixon.

"The description matches one of our unknowns from the Tall Indian motel," Nate went on.

"We're on our way," Olmstead said, and was about to hang up.

Nate caught him just before he signed off.

"And Buck, one more thing."

Nate had just spotted the two Feds coming into Olmstead's outer office, asking Becky for the sheriff. "They're here for him."

"Okay," Olmstead said.

He didn't look at LaCrosse.

They were stopped at the light at the intersection facing the sheriff's office. Olmstead tapped on the steering wheel. LaCrosse hadn't failed to notice that the sheriff's clear preoccupation with something had begun just after the phone call from Nate.

When the signal changed, Olmstead didn't react.

"Light's green," LaCrosse said.

Olmstead snapped out of his daze and drove across the street into the parking lot.

From the window beside her desk, Becky could see the sheriff's car pull up to the curb.

"They're here," she told Nate.

"Thank God," he said.

As Becky went back to watching through the blinds, Olmstead put the car in park.

He didn't kill the engine, though.

Instead he just sat there for a moment, staring straight ahead as LaCrosse cracked the side door.

But LaCrosse didn't get out. He looked over his shoulder, then sat back.

"You okay?" he asked.

Olmstead took a second to think.

Then he told LaCrosse to close the door.

Becky turned from the window to Nate. The car was now pulling back out of the lot amid the squeals of overstressed tire rubber.

"They're leaving!" she told Nate.

Nate crossed quickly to the window in time to see the sheriff's vehicle tear up the road.

At that moment the door opened and Special Agent Montgomery, one of the FBI delegation who'd come down from Dallas, stuck his head inside the office.

Montgomery had decided to personally oversee that LaCrosse was taken into custody. Frank was a loose cannon and he wanted to make sure there were no more problems with him.

"What's the story, Deputy?" he asked Nate. "You said he'd be here fifteen minutes ago."

"Well, maybe they had some car trouble," Nate covered. "We'll try again."

He picked up the phone and started punching up the number of Olmstead's cell phone. Montgomery didn't wait for Nate to finish dialing.

Disgusted, he wheeled around and strode from the office, back into the anteroom.

"Buck?" Nate said, "what the hell's going on?" he asked.

The circus lights atop the sheriff's car revolved and the vehicle's siren blared. Olmstead held the phone with one hand and turned the steering wheel with the other.

"Don't ask any questions if you don't want to hear the answer," Buck cautioned his deputy.

"Buck, are you out of your mind?" Nate shot back. "You're interfering with a Federal investigation. In case you forgot, that's called obstruction of justice."

"I damn well know what it's called," Olmstead said to him. "Just get on the phone to the airport and have the chopper ready in ten minutes."

"A department helicopter?" Nate asked.

"And have a car waiting in Martinsburg," Buck added.

"McGinnis will have a field day when he hears about this. Even if you win, he'll have you impeached."

"Then consider this my last official act," Olmstead told him, and hit the Talk button, terminating the call.

Nate racked the receiver, looking past Becky at the closed door separating them from the waiting agents in the anteroom.

"Call the airport," Nate told her, resigning himself to the trouble he knew lay dead ahead. "Tell Sam to get the chopper ready. Tell him that I told you to." He picked up his coat and hat as she dialed.

"Where are you going?" she asked.

"Out to vote, get a cold one, and consider what I'm going to do when I get out of prison," he told her, and headed for the door.

Olmstead stood at the deputy's desk in the Amarillo Airport Sheriff's substation. From the helipad outside came the earsplitting hydraulic scream of a police chopper's blades. They were beginning to spin up to torque as the rotorcraft's engines warmed up.

"Colorado Highway Patrol says they've got

roadblocks up in a two hundred mile radius," Olmstead said to LaCrosse. "A lot of snow up there; slow damn going. Maybe you'll get lucky." Olmstead put out his hand. "Time's a'wasting, Frank," he said.

They shook, and both men felt the emotion of what was happening. Olmstead was putting it all on the line. Not just for LaCrosse. But for an abstract thing that, for want of a better word, might be called justice.

Saying no more, the sheriff turned and walked toward the door. LaCrosse watched him leave.

"Buck," he said. "Wait a minute."

Olmstead stopped and spun around, realizing that for the first time since he'd known him, LaCrosse had called him by name.

"Thanks."

Olmstead permitted himself a smile. Coming from LaCrosse, it was practically a song of praise. Olmstead touched his two front fingers to his hat brim and went out the door.

Minutes later, he stood by his car watching the police chopper lift off the helipad, climb to its cruising altitude of sixty feet, and vector west.

He followed it awhile with his eyes, then climbed back in the car.

14

With his coat balled up under his head as a makeshift pillow, Lane leaned against the window of the Caddy, fast asleep.

Bob watched him from behind the wheel as he drove the Eldorado up a winding mountain road piled high with windblown drifts and plowed-up palisades on either side.

Lane came awake and began rubbing his arms. It was cold. Damn cold. Too cold, in fact. When he looked over at Bob, he realized that Bob now had his coat on.

"Heater ain't working," Bob explained. "Radio too. Shorty must've blown a fuse when he was working on 'er."

To prove his point, Bob flipped the heat control button a couple of times. No fan. No heat. Nothing.

Lane put on his own coat and sat shivering in it and blowing on his hands. He watched the car begin to negotiate a series of sharp switchback turns above a sheer drop of maybe a hundred feet.

"Where are we?" he asked, looking back at Bob.

"Little shortcut of mine," Bob told him. "We skirt the storm this way. It'll cut two hours off our time."

Just as he spoke those words, the front tires rolled over an ice patch and the Caddy went into a long skid. Bob quickly pulled clear of it, though.

"*If* we get there," Lane added.

"Trust me, Doc," Bob told him, waving off Lane's concern. "Trust me."

Lane nodded and went back to watching the scenery roll by. After a minute or two Bob turned to him.

"Doc, while you were sleeping I was thinking, and I decided I have to ask a great favor of you."

"Sure," Lane answered, hearing the gravity in Bob's voice.

"You told me a secret," he began. "It's my turn now." Bob collected himself and went on. "I have a son. I'm not the best old man he could've had, but I do my best. I have someone to keep him for me."

"Where's his mother?" asked Lane.

"She's dead," Bob said.

Lane thought about this.

"Why are you telling me this?" he wanted to know.

"I've been thinking about . . ."—Bob groped for words—"if something happened to me, he's got no one to look up to."

"Nothing's gonna happen to you," Lane countered.

"It's not like I'm asking you to take care of him," Bob explained. "He just needs someone to sort of be a godfather to him, to be an example."

"Me?" Lane asked with shock.

But he could see that Bob was serious.

"You're smart, Doc. Tough. Responsible. Hard qualities to find these days. Anyway, if something did happen to me, I'd appreciate it if you'd do that for me."

"Sure," Lane agreed. What else could he say?

"Thank you," Bob told him, sounding relieved. "He lives in Oakland. Eighty-eight, ninety-nine Todd Street. Down near the bay. You remember that address?"

"Eighty-eight, ninety-nine Todd," Lane repeated.

"Thanks Doc," Bob said, nodding at Lane and smiling. "I feel better already."

The Caddy gave a jolt as it went into another skid. Bob quickly turned into it, and after a moment that made the road seem even thinner than it was, the tires found a hold on the snow-swept asphalt and the car straightened out again.

"Just in the nick of time, huh?" Bob said.

They both began to laugh, but it was nervous laughter.

A moment later, as the car went into another hairpin turn, it went scudding toward the precipice.

Neither of them was laughing anymore as Bob pumped the brakes and the car picked up speed instead, skidding sideways.

"Goddammit! Get out!" Bob hollered.

It was obvious by this time that Lane's side would go over first.

He was already scrabbling for the door latch.

The door opened easily, but his seat-belt catch was stuck. As he tore at it, Lane looked up to see nothing but vista.

Then the Caddy slammed into the thin snow embankment on the roadside and vanished over the edge.

It sailed into space like a ghost, making hardly any sound except for the eerie whoosh of dislodged, falling snow, and plummeted thirty feet onto a snow-covered outcrop directly below the roadway.

The Caddy finally came to rest on its side, held by a tree mere feet from a second drop that would have plunged it a hundred feet more to the canyon floor below.

Lane came back to his senses, realizing that he wasn't inside the car anymore. He was lying on his face in the snow, a couple of yards down the road. Snow was in his eyes. His mouth. His nostrils. His ears.

Yet he seemed to be all in one piece; at least there was no blood that he could see.

Getting to his feet shakily, Lane looked around him.

There was no sign of the car.

He trudged to the edge of the steep incline and spotted it below him.

"Bob!" he called out. "Hey, Bob!"

Getting no answer, Lane started down the snow-covered embankment, sending a snow slide toward the Caddy below.

Crabbing sideways a little, he finally caught sight of Bob through the shattered passenger window. He was pinned behind the steering wheel. Lane only got a few feet further before he heard Bob call out to him from the car.

"Don't come down here, Doc!" he warned. "It's too dangerous. One wrong move and they'll be digging both our asses out in July."

"Can you get out?" Lane hollered back.

Lane saw Bob struggle to free himself, only to fall back helplessly. It looked like he was trapped in his position by the wheel.

"I'm coming down," Lane called out, determined to help his friend whatever the cost.

"No, stay up there!" Bob shouted angrily.

He hadn't been fooling around when he'd warned Lane of trouble.

But Lane ignored him. Bob might be seriously injured. It wasn't right to just leave him there.

Lane had to see what he could do.

"Goddamn, you deaf son-of-a-bitch!" Bob shouted at him again. "I told you to stay the hell up there!"

But Lane had already plodded through the treacherous blanket of snow and was at the broken window.

Looking down at Bob, Lane remarked, "This ain't so bad."

But Lane was talking to himself, trying to forget the gut-wrenching drop just beyond Bob's head. He carefully climbed up on the side of the car and worked his way through the passenger window, slowly easing himself down over the passenger seat until he was nearly vertical, his legs sticking straight out into the wind. His left elbow, jammed against Bob's seat, and his hip, which rested on the passenger seat, held his weight precariously. Lane paused to steady himself.

"As long as you're down here, we might as well get me out of this," Bob said.

"Just hold still," Lane ordered. Up close, he saw that it was the harness that was actually holding Bob inside. It had gotten caught on the seat lever and become badly snarled. Lane reached up into his back pocket and fished out his pocket knife.

He gave it to Bob to unfold, who then returned it so Lane could saw through the harness.

With a snap the harness finally gave, sending the car into a terrifying spasm. But once it ceased quivering, Bob was able to climb up and out of the car, using Lane as a makeshift ladder. Then he helped pull Lane out.

"Thanks, Doc," Bob said, starting up the slope. "Let's get the hell out of here." Lane started after him.

But then Lane looked back and spotted his pack. It was just sitting there on the rear seat. And it looked so easy to get. He just had to try to pull it out before they left the Caddy for good. All his stuff was in there.

While Bob continued trudging cautiously up-slope, Lane went plodding back to the car. Reaching it without mishap, he climbed back through the open window and struggled to reach the pack, shaking the car and dislodging clumps of snow under it.

He finally just managed to touch one of the straps of his pack. Yeah, now he had it! Giving a quick buck, he pulled himself and the pack out of the car. With a smile of satisfaction and triumph, he turned back to the roadway above and saw that Bob had turned back and seen him. Lane held up his pack to show Bob that it was alright.

Suddenly the hard-packed snow and the lone tree supporting the Caddy tore loose from the outcrop, taking the car with it.

Surprised, Lane found himself dragged down to his knees and sliding, his arms flailing uselessly. But, as if they had minds of their own, his feet somehow recovered and quickly dug into what solid snow they could find. Lane made a tentative attempt to stand, and when that seemed too dangerous, grabbed at a now exposed root for stability.

"Doc!" Bob shouted and began a wild, headlong plunge down through the snowdrifts toward Lane and the lip of the precipice.

With such a terrible drop so close, Lane didn't want to wait. He pulled on the root and for a moment worked his way up the slope. Then the root cracked like a couple of rifle shots and finally broke, sending Lane somersaulting backward over the cliff.

Lane reached out wildly as he went over, clawing, grasping, clutching at any twig to stop his plunge toward death, yet closing only on empty air.

He knew in a moment that he would never make it. That he was finished.

And then to his surprise his hand closed around something jutting from the edge of the cliff—a sapling, rooted in the rocky soil and freed from the cold embrace of the encircling snow.

Lane clutched it with all his might as his feet swung over the edge into thin air. He looked down to see the Eldorado smashed on the jagged boulders rising out of the ravine below.

Lane looked up again. A wave of adrenaline-fed terror coursed through him as he felt the bark of the young tree begin to give and slough off under his glove.

"Bob!" he shouted, hoping against hope that his friend would have made it down to him somehow. But there was no answer, and as Lane's hand slipped even further, he knew that it had been foolish to have thought of help.

"*Jesus, no,*" he cried out, realizing that he was going to die. That death was only a second or two away, and that nothing in heaven or earth would stop it from swallowing him up.

Then the bark tore away completely and Lane started to fall.

Then a gloved hand reached down suddenly and grabbed Lane by the arm, holding on to him with an iron grip.

Looking up, Lane saw Bob, bracing himself between a large rock and the sapling he'd been holding on to.

Then, with his other hand now firmly

around him, Bob began pulling up Lane and his dangling pack.

Bob stood looking over the cliff where the Caddy had been visible only a few minutes before. Lane was sitting by the side of the road, his head in his hands. He still couldn't believe he was alive.

"You know, pardner," Bob said to Lane, "I think you've had enough risk to last you a lifetime."

He put out his hand and Lane stared at it.

"Maybe you're right," he said, and took Bob's hand to let his friend help him to his feet.

Maybe it was the stress of the accident, but a shudder of some nameless fear ran through Lane as he looked around at the vast, foreboding mountain range.

Darkness would be coming soon, he realized.

The fact that the snow had at least temporarily stopped didn't do anything to calm him either. Lane shook off the terror and shouldered his pack.

"I hope you know where we are," he told Bob.

But Bob was grinning.

"I sure do, pardner," he told Lane. "I surely do."

He clapped Lane on the shoulder and

turned to walk down the cold, deserted road, Lane at his side in the gathering twilight.

"Just a little stroll," Bob said reassuringly. "Then a nice warm bed."

15

FBI Special Agent Grant Montgomery stood outside one of the cells in the Amarillo lockup.

He'd lost one prisoner, that was true.

But what the Lord taketh away He also giveth.

Montgomery had himself a new prisoner.

The man sitting on the edge of the bunk behind the row of iron bars had just crossed one line too many, and Montgomery would make damn sure he was punished.

That man was Buck Olmstead.

"Don't even think about trying to pull some local strings here, Sheriff," Montgomery cautioned the man in the cell. "I consider what you did to be a serious obstruction of justice. And I'm going to make sure you remember this stay."

Olmstead smiled back at him.

"Damn, Grant, you got me quaking in my boots," he said.

Montgomery tried to smile back. But his

smile faltered, then faded away completely.

His gambit checked, the Fed turned on his heels and walked down the cellblock corridor.

Let that sucker stew for a while, he thought. Montgomery promised himself that the last laugh would belong to him.

Yellow mylar tape bearing the words *Police Line Do Not Cross* was strung from orange-and-black plastic pylons, cordoning off Shorty's Gas Station from the street. Red and blue police lights strobed across the old garage's redbrick walls. And two-way tranceivers squawked unintelligibly. No one was listening anyway.

Nearby, the crew of a remote-uplink television van was setting up the vehicle's microwave dish, aiming it at a satellite in orbit one hundred miles above. They were awaiting the arrival of a TV reporter from one of the network stations. The story had begun to break nationally.

It was finally news.

Frank LaCrosse raised a section of yellow crime-scene tape and slipped under the cordon. Flashing his credentials at a deputy posted to stand guard, he was directed to the garage's office.

Inside, LaCrosse found the familiar organized chaos of cops and medical-examiner staff involved in the investigation of a murder scene. Most of the preliminary forensic work had already been done, though.

The area had been dusted for fingerprints, physical evidence had been collected, tagged and bagged, and crime-scene photographs had been taken. At this stage, most of the traffic inside the garage was made up of nonessential personnel.

As LaCrosse came inside, people began filing out, leaving LaCrosse alone with a Highway Patrol officer whose uniform bore a captain's insignia.

"Mr. LaCrosse?" the state trooper asked the newcomer.

"That's right."

"Captain Heber, Colorado State Police. They said you were coming. I'm supposed to hold you till your people get up here tomorrow."

"Mind if I look around anyway, Captain?" LaCrosse asked, not surprised to hear this.

"Be my guest." He had told Montgomery he would make sure LaCrosse didn't leave. He didn't tell the arrogant Fed he would babysit.

Heber directed LaCrosse through the cluttered office to the doorway of the small bathroom.

"Victim's name was Clyde 'Shorty' Callahan," Heber said. The body lay sprawled in a pool of blood before the sink. "He died of—"

"Knife wound in the femoral artery," La-Crosse interjected.

Heber blinked and flashed LaCrosse a telling look.

"Yeah, that's right," he said. "No murder weapon was found, but we did find this on the victim, though."

Heber pointed at Shorty's holster still at his hip. "We've bagged and tagged the firearm, but it was still snapped in place under the body when we arrived. It looks like he never even tried to pull it."

Frank took a long look at Shorty, then moved back into the office. There he noticed the railroad map on one of the walls. His eye also took in an assortment of cheap framed family snapshots, a few stuffed animal heads and unimpressive racks of antlers.

Then he noticed something that made him pause.

It was a railroad calendar on which Shorty had religiously crossed off each day of the month with an X.

Every single day, right up until the seventeenth, had been crossed off. But the next day, February 18, that day had been circled.

LaCrosse's mind raced back to the numerals on the bottom of the photo of his abducted child—2/18.

"You must kill me to find him," LaCrosse

repeated in a barely audible whisper, saying aloud the words on the back of the photograph.

"What's that?" asked Heber, not having caught any of it.

"Nothing," LaCrosse told him, still staring at the calendar. "Nothing important."

"Kind of got ahead of himself, didn't he?" Heber remarked, following LaCrosse's gaze. "Not even the seventeenth yet."

"That's right," LaCrosse answered, and changed the subject. "Any word on the car?"

"No," said Heber. "We still have roadblocks out on Routes 10, 160, and 350. If you want to get out of this valley, you'd have to pass through one of them—and that Cadillac hasn't gone through."

LaCrosse now turned his attention back to Shorty's railroad map. His eye traced the fine red lines demarcating secondary roads.

"What about the roads up in the mountains?" he asked. "Have they been checked?"

"Don't need to," Heber returned. "I can tell you right now, they're completely impassable. Nothing going in or out."

LaCrosse gave Heber a half-nod in acknowledgment as he returned to study the map. There was something there. It was right in front of him, but he couldn't see it. Yet.

"If you don't think he bypassed the roadblocks," he thought aloud, "and he's not in the mountains, then where is he?"

"I didn't say the car didn't make it *through* the roadblocks," Heber countered. "I said no *Cadillac* matching the description's gone through."

Heber paused to consider what he wanted to say for a moment, then went on.

"Look, Mr. LaCrosse, I've got a report that says we've got over two hundred stranded vehicles on I-25 alone. And that's just between here and Pueblo. If they're heading toward Salida, the weather's even worse. See what I mean?"

LaCrosse nodded. He'd caught the gist of it. The trail was cold.

"I think that when we finally get around to digging all those cars out," Heber concluded, "we're gonna find us a white Cadillac."

LaCrosse and Heber walked past the police cordon and out into the snow-covered street. The building was now lit by incandescent floods as the remote location crew taped the reporter filing her story for the eleven o'clock news.

Most of the curious had already left. So had most of the cops. The street was beginning to take on the forlorn look of a circus whose tents have just been struck.

"Your people were pretty adamant about

locking you up, Mr. LaCrosse," Heber told him. "But seeing as it's twenty miles to the nearest lockup, I asked Ruth to hold a room for you across the street."

He nodded at the single-story maintenance way station next to the railroad tracks. It was an unassuming building but better by far than any jail.

"I figure if the killer can't get out of here," Heber told LaCrosse with a smile, "you won't either."

"Thanks Captain."

"Don't thank me," Heber corrected. "Thank Buck Olmstead. You got a good friend there."

LaCrosse nodded his agreement. Buck Olmstead had indeed turned out to be his friend, and a man of principle besides.

Heber pulled up his coat collar against the increasing cold. It was getting late and a high-pressure front was beginning to sweep in from the mountains. It was going to be a long, cold night.

Heber turned to leave.

"Damn shame about that election," he told LaCrosse, almost as an afterthought. "Won't be the same without him."

LaCrosse didn't answer.

He started for the railroad dorm.

The lanky woman in her midfifties got up from behind the desk where she and a gray-haired man in a faded maroon cardigan watched a basketball game on a small television set. She smiled at the visitor.

"Howdy. You Mr. LaCrosse?"

He nodded.

"Sign in here," she told him.

LaCrosse began to sign, hearing Ruth tell him, "Terrible thing, that murder. You know, I used to baby-sit for Shorty when he was a little feller. I just can't believe it."

The piercing single note of a diesel horn came suddenly from the night outside the way station walls.

LaCrosse stopped writing and listened as the train gave another blast on the whistle.

He stared through the lobby window at the tracks not more than forty feet away, where a diesel locomotive was being readied for a snow-clearing run. Attached to its front was a large anvil-shaped snowplow.

"On their way up to clear the pass," Ruth remarked.

LaCrosse didn't answer.

Lost in thought, he watched and listened as the engineer tooted the horn one more time and his assistant came running out of the station and swung aboard. Then the black leviathan began to roll slowly forward and into the enveloping darkness.

Ruth's voice pulled him back from his thoughts. "Shorty used to do that," she said.

"His wife made him give it up on account it was too dangerous. That's irony, isn't it? He gave up clearing passes because it was too dangerous, then gets hisself killed in his own garage."

She shook her head, turned to pull a key from a pigeonhole behind her, and set it on the counter. "First room on the left," she said. "Enjoy your stay."

Light filled the room, chasing away the darkness. The room was small and sparsely furnished with two bunk-style beds, two wash basins, two mirrors, and one clothes closet.

A real railroad man's hotel room, Bob thought as he shut the door behind him and looked around, remembering his previous stays at the Eagle Hotel in the town of La Veta, Colorado.

He headed straight for the sink to wash up while Lane went to the bunk against the wall to lay down.

"Where is everyone, Al?" Bob said to the hotel manager, who had come in ahead of them and now stood to one side. Bob knew Al from way back. "I thought this place would be packed."

Bob unwrapped a small bar of vanity soap and began washing up. Al leaned against the door frame and chewed on a wood-stem match.

"You can't get in and you can't get out," he

said. "So it ain't packed. How'd y'all get in anyway?"

"We hoofed it. Had a little car trouble up on the mountain," Bob explained, patting his face dry with a large white towel.

"You're lucky," said Al, and nodded at Lane who was already snoring. "Don't look like he held up too well," he commented.

Bob hung the towel back up and looked over at his friend.

"He did better than you think," he said to the manager in a tone that brooked no argument.

16

Olmstead watched Robby Nugent collect his
dinner tray from the bunk in the cell. He could
recall feeding Robby one of his world-famous
BLT specials once; now Robby was returning
the favor, albeit in his official capacity as the
Amarillo lockup's jailer.

"Damn good chicken à la king," he told the
uniformed deputy as he handed him his coffee
cup. "You tell Sally that, hear?"

"Will do, Sheriff," Robby said, and dis-
creetly placed a small brown paper bag on the
table in front of Olmstead. "And I brought
that little something else you asked for."

Olmstead thanked him and asked for a couple of glasses too.

Nugent said he'd be right back with them
and went out, leaving the cell door wide open.

Olmstead opened the bag and took out a
pint of charcoal-filtered Kentucky sour mash.
It was the brand whose label always reminded

him of Thanksgiving, the best kind for sipping.

"I see you're adjusting well to your new situation."

Olmstead heard a voice and looked up. Nate stood outside the bars.

"Come on in," Olmstead told him. "Care to join the recently unemployed in a drink?"

Nate went in and sank onto the bunk, followed by Robby, who'd brought up the rear carrying two pony glasses.

Olmstead took the glasses and set them down. Unscrewing the cap he looked back at Nate, who wore the mantle of dejection like other men wore ten-dollar ties.

"Don't get so down, Nate. It's not your fault," he told his chief deputy.

"I just can't help thinking that maybe if we'd made that announcement, things would have gone differently."

Olmstead poured a healthy slug.

"Maybe," he said. "Or maybe if he'd killed in Midland instead of Amarillo or if Saldez had had his shoot-em-up in our jurisdiction instead of McGinnis's . . ." He let his voice trail off and finished pouring. "Who knows?" he concluded, setting the bottle back down.

"Or maybe you should've turned him in," Nate reflected.

"Maybe I should have done lots of things differently, Nate," Olmstead countered, handing the deputy one of the glasses, "but turning Frank in was never an option."

They clinked glasses and began working on the bourbon, Olmstead in one of the cell's two chairs, his foot on the other.

"Why not?" Nate asked after a moment.

"Because he was telling the truth," Olmstead answered, "and once you've heard the truth, everything else is just cheap whiskey."

Nate stared at the floor.

"I might have settled for that much," he said softly.

"No you wouldn't have," retorted Olmstead. "You're a good cop, Nate. You're going to do fine with Jack. We both knew that sooner or later my run was gonna be over."

Olmstead took another sip and swallowed the mellow Kentucky moonshine.

"Now go home, hug your kids, kiss that pretty wife of yours, and know that what you did was the right thing."

Nate thought that over a minute, sipping his drink.

"What about you?"

"Me? Well, you can see that this whole experience has devastated me," Olmstead answered.

Grinning, he put his other foot up on the chair and poured himself another shot, thinking that it was getting to feel more and more like Thanksgiving with every drink he took.

* * *

The bearded bartender at the railroad diner ran a rag around the rim of the shot glass he held up to the light. When he hung it back up amid scores of others on the overhead rack, there was somebody waiting to be served.

"Bob!" he shouted out amiably, going over to the patron. "Damn good seeing you!"

"You too, Hank," Bob told him, smiling one of his toothy smiles that sprawled across the bottom third of his lean cowboy's face. "Whiskey, straight up."

"Comin' right atcha," Hank said, and went to get the bottle.

Looking across the room, Bob saw two attractive women seated at a table adjacent to the bar.

One in particular, a blonde with an agreeable shape that her sweater and shearling jacket gave tantalizing hints of, caught his eye.

Bob turned on the charm and flashed another one of his all-purpose surefire smiles in her direction, but she didn't seem the least interested. The lady turned back to her girlfriend and pretended Bob didn't exist.

Bob shrugged and took a seat over toward the middle of the bar, beside two veteran railroad men he recognized.

Cubby and Tate looked pretty much like they'd looked when he'd last seen them.

Cubby, a brakeman, and Tate, an engineer,

were nursing beers and coffee as they watched the late news on the wall-mounted TV in the crotch of the wall to the right of the bar.

"What's shakin', Cubby?" Bob asked, sidling onto the stool next to the brakeman.

"Somebody killed over in Martinsburg," Cubby answered as Hank came over with Bob's whiskey, then went back to the other end of the bar, took out another shot glass, and started polishing.

Bob turned his attention to the TV screen on which the remote van's camera crew had caught LaCrosse and Heber during a fast pan. "They think it might be the same guy from Amarillo?" Bob commented.

"If they do, they ain't saying," Tate told him. "Colorado police say they're looking for a young man."

The news wrapped up and the sports anchor came on. Bob lost interest and turned back to the two ladies at the adjacent table.

The blonde was looking his way again but still avoiding direct eye contact. Still giving him the cold shoulder. But she was warming to him, Bob thought, and that was a fact.

"Well," Bob said to the railroad men, turning back to the bar, "you boys seem to be up on all the latest news."

"Well, hell," Cubby returned sourly, "been stuck here since day before yesterday. Haven't done a thing but sit around and watch the damn TV."

Bob nodded but his mind was elsewhere. On the blonde to be precise.

He watched her stand and put on her coat. Once more he tried to beam some charm her way, but his smile still lit no raging fires.

Shaking his head at what might have been, Bob watched both women walk right out the door. A quick scan of the place told him it would be all stag from there on in. Nothing but railroaders in the bar.

"Well, then it's time we get that pass opened up and move on," Bob told Tate as he downed the rest of his whiskey. "What do you say, Tate?"

"Gonna send a crew up tonight," he answered with a nod. "You're welcome to go along with 'em. Be like old times."

"In my youth, friend," Bob said. "In my youth."

The three of them shared a laugh at that remark. Then Bob stood up and dug some bills out of his pocket, laying them flat on the bar and setting his glass on top of them.

"Thanks, Hank," he called to the bartender, fixing to leave.

"What's your rush?" Hank said.

"Your lack of female clientele disturbs me," Bob told him.

"Ain't we good enough for you?" Hank retorted.

Bob slid on his canhart jacket over his red down vest.

"No offense, Hank," he answered, "but one smile from a willin' woman's worth ten from a friendly barkeep."

He patted Cubby on the back.

"By the way," he said to Tate, "what do you hear about the two-eighteen?"

"Out of Martinsburg?" Tate returned. "Last I heard it's going over, but it don't come here, you know."

"I know," Bob replied. He pretty much had figured that the freight wouldn't stop in La Veta. He just wanted to make sure of it. "Just asking."

With a final wave to the three of them, Bob turned and headed out the door into the darkness.

The cold was bitter in the extreme, and the wind was like something stropped to a wicked edge.

Bob pulled his collar up around his ears and stared down the road through a cloud of his vaporized breath. No question about it, Bob thought just then.

He knew exactly where to go on a bad night like this.

* * *

The blonde from the La Veta diner reached behind her back and unfastened the hooks of her black brassiere. She dropped it to the floor beside her denim skirt. She removed her panties and thick wool socks with swift, precise movements. Then she gathered the clothes together and crossed her neat, simple bedroom. At the closet she bent to stuff them into a hamper. As she did, her breasts swayed beneath her, and it was this movement that reminded her of the cold outside and the unshaded window beside her that anyone could look through.

With a quick glance she noticed no one watching, though, and pulled the shade down. Nonetheless, the blonde pulled her thick green bathrobe off her bedpost and quickly wrapped herself in it. Then she took the sweater she'd laid on the bed, folded it across her chest and carefully replaced it on a shelf in the closet.

Standing in front of the window again, the blonde made a check of the room. She ran her hand across the bedspread to smooth it, then went out to her bath.

She liked things just so when she went to bed.

Outside, watching her silhouette, a shadow broke away from the darkness and entered the dim light that eluded the shade.

Damn fine figure, Bob thought to himself as he silently drew up to the rear of the house.

*   *   *

Water ran in the tub.

Steam filled the small tiled bathroom.

She tested the temperature with her hand. It was just right.

With the tap still running, she eased herself into the tub and let it fill.

Then, leaning back and reaching toward the soap dish, she turned the faucet knob with the big toe of her left foot.

Bob tested the knob of the house's rear door.

It was a cheap lock, a twenty-dollar hardware store lock, and he wouldn't have even needed a credit card to open it.

Had it been locked.

Bob smiled and strode into the dark interior.

Silently closing the door behind him, Bob crossed the kitchen and went to the parlor in front.

Near the stairway landing he paused, listening.

Diffused light spilled from the upper story and there was the sound of rushing water.

Treading softly, he began to climb the flight of carpeted steps.

Reaching the upper story, he passed the lighted bedroom, moving toward the closed bathroom door.

*   *   *

Her head tilted back against the rim of the tub, the woman felt the relaxing warmth seep inside her.

She closed her eyes and began to daydream.

Hawaii.

Java.

Places without train whistles.

She was caught up so fully that she was completely unaware that the bathroom door was slowly opening behind her—until a hinge creaked and she turned suddenly, her eyes wide with surprise.

The banshee wail of a diesel horn from a freight train juddering past on the rail line jerked Frank awake from a dream in which he was a rodeo cowboy riding something huge, black, and demonic. The beast breathed fire and bellowed as it tried to throw him to the ground, and its cries sounded like a diesel horn, and the sound pierced LaCrosse's brain like a long, sharp needle.

He held on to the reigns as best he could, desperately trying to stay mounted long enough to tame the beast, but slipping farther along its side with each passing second.

Finally LaCrosse could hold on no longer. The beast sensed this too and, with a savage lunge of his body, succeeded in flinging its rider off.

LaCrosse went spinning through a vortex of

swirling, pinwheeling yellow, screaming in fear as he tumbled down on what he knew was to be an endless fall into deeper and deeper nothingness.

Then he found himself as always, sitting up in bed, bathed in sweat as cold and slick as mercury, breathing hard and fast.

At first he could not remember where he was. Then he became frightened. The bed was vibrating as if it were the earth trembling.

Then he remembered.

He got up, still dressed, and walked outside into the cold night. He stared at the rail yard less than twenty feet away.

A freight train, whose flatcars and boxcars stretched from the darkness on his left to the darkness on his right, lumbered past. At first Frank thought it was its passage that made the ground beneath his feet shudder. Then he realized it was what was written on the side of each car that was making his legs shiver as he processed it: the lighted number "2-18."

Suddenly he was aware that there was another person standing on the porch beside him.

LaCrosse turned to see that it was Ruth, the hotel owner.

Wearing a terry-cloth robe, she wrapped her arms tightly around herself to ward off the night's chill.

"Well, they got the pass open," she said.

The final cars of the outbound train were just passing into the darkness. Ruth wrapped her robe more tightly around her and turned to go back in.

"Don't worry," she told LaCrosse, figuring she knew why he couldn't sleep. Noise of those boxcars could wake the dead, 'specially if you weren't used to it. "The two-eighteen's the only train till tomorrow."

The tires skidded in the snow as the car took a tight, sudden turn. LaCrosse fought to regain control, feathering the brakes to stabilize the vehicle. He accelerated again as he came out of the turn and the road changed into a straightaway, parallel to the course of the railway tracks.

Directly in front of him, less than a mile now, he could see the train that had just left the station. It was moving faster now than it had been on its outbound course from the yard, but not as fast as he was driving.

LaCrosse floored the accelerator until the digital needle on the speedometer panel climbed into the red zone.

He didn't care. His entire being was fixed on overtaking the freight train, then passing it, and then boarding it, and he would do it even if it cost him his life.

The road began to descend now, angling down to a riverbank; then it turned, followed a streambed, and passed the railway trestle spanning the river, over which the train would soon be going.

LaCrosse followed the turn, meaning to stop, but he'd misjudged the angle and the car began fishtailing into an uncontrolled skid. Nothing LaCrosse tried succeeded in pulling it out. It went slamming sideways through a snowbank, and careened into the river, coming to rest half-submerged on its side.

LaCrosse climbed out. He was unharmed, and the train was coming steadily down the line, already beginning to approach the trestle.

In the headlight beams of his immobilized vehicle, LaCrosse checked his Sig Sauer and lurched through the icy water to head it off.

Reaching the track bed as the first cars began rolling over the trestle, he started running alongside the slow-moving train.

He knew that even if he succeeded in gaining a grip on one of the metal handholds extending from the boxcars, he would have to hug tight against the side of the car as it went over the bridge or risk being clipped by the bridge beams and knocked into the swirling waters of the ravine far below.

Picking up speed, LaCrosse trotted at a loping run as the middle cars began to lumber toward the bridge. He reached out for one of the ladders on a boxcar, but the train was moving faster than he thought.

For a moment, he hung free in space before falling hard to the ground, just inches from the rails and the rolling wheels.

As if to protest his effort, the steel wheels gave a horrible shriek.

Frank jumped up and started running, but the last of the coal cars toward the rear of the train was already rushing by him.

He had no chance to grab one. And he realized that he was fast running out of time and chances. The trestle was looming up ahead of him, and the train would soon be completely past him.

He leaped for the first railing on the caboose, just touching it, but his near miss held him back from gripping it tight enough. His hand slipped free, and Frank did all he could to keep from falling again.

Now the rear platform was his only chance. Steeling himself and running as fast he could with freezing wet legs over uneven ground, Frank stretched out for the metal rail. His fingers wrapped around the bar and he could feel himself get pulled out of his stride and off the ground. He jumped forward to get a grip with his other hand, then threw his legs at the icy platform.

Dangling there, feet flailing, the caboose started over the trestle.

Drawing up his left foot, he managed to hook his toe between two of the metal boarding steps depending from the platform.

Now he raised his right foot too, meaning to place both feet on the steps.

But this time his toe struck a wooden railroad tie, sending a jolt of pain up his ankle as he mounted the steps and scrambled onto the platform.

There he took a few moments to catch his breath.

He realized the he had torn his shoe and sent it tumbling into the river. It was a small price to pay, though. LaCrosse was thankful to be alive.

Holding on to the railing of the juddering, swaying caboose, LaCrosse was too winded to do much but look out at the view from the rear of the train.

In the distance, he watched the headlights of his car grow smaller and dimmer, and then disappear entirely, as the train carried him farther and higher into the mountains.

17

The heat of the oven warmed her face.

She felt the warm air currents lift up strands of her blonde hair as she pulled open the door and slid out the stainless-steel baking sheet with mittened hands.

The biscuits were done just right—slightly brown on top, tender along the sides. He would like them.

Working quickly before they cooled much more, she placed a few of the biscuits on a white china plate, spread them with raspberry jam and, licking her fingers, carried the plate and two mugs of steaming black coffee out of the kitchen on a wooden serving tray.

Crossing the hall, she went into her bathroom without knocking.

Bob sat soaking in the tub and watched her come in. Damned if she wasn't surprised when she'd seen him sneak up on her last night.

The hem of her robe lifted momentarily as

she set the breakfast tray down on the sink and put Bob's coffee down on the edge of the tub. Bob feasted his eyes on the flash of silken-smooth thigh that was revealed.

Then she sat down atop the toilet seat, sipping her coffee and watching Bob take his bath.

"You know, I really don't do this anymore," she said.

"What?" Bob returned, "serve your guests breakfast in the tub?"

"You know what I mean," she told him.

"Honey, we are what we are," Bob said with a smile.

She looked down, abashed, as Bob took the scrub brush to his back and glanced her way.

"Don't worry," he told her, "I won't be coming back."

Her head snapped back up at this and her consternation was evident. She and Bob might have had a good thing going.

"I like that," Bob said to her, "I like being missed."

Shadows in a sunbeam wavered on the ceiling. Lane watched them in a stupor of half-wakefulness, watching the dark things dance inside the light.

For a heartbeat they spelled out something to him, but then the moment passed and Lane was wide awake and sitting on the edge of his bunk, running his fingers through his hair and rubbing the sleep from the corners of his eyes.

Yawning, he reached for his pack, lifting it from the floor near the side of the bunk; then he rummaged around inside for his shaving kit.

As usual, the thing he wanted was at the bottom, and he had to put everything else back again, including the Colt pistol, which he replaced last of all.

Lane then got up and went out into the hall, idly noticing that the morning sun had shifted and the light on the ceiling was already gone.

The Eagle Hotel's bathroom was a throwback to a bygone age, when pioneer notions of privacy still were the norm. It was as huge as a dormitory, with six sinks, six showers, and eight shower stalls.

It was already late in the morning for the railroad men who made up virtually all of the Eagle's clientele, and the bathroom was crowded and noisy.

Lane found a free sink where he first softened his beard with hot water and shave cream, then rasped off the overnight stubble with a twin-edged disposable razor.

After finishing up, he went over to a shower stall that had just become available, turned on the tap, and savored the hot spray exploding against his back.

As Lane turned to run the shower on his

chest, he caught a sudden fragment of conversation from what he first thought was the stall to his right.

The words were clearly audible, even with the water going and the hubbub in the bathroom.

"I know what I'm talking about," said one of the voices. "Yeah, a Cadillac."

"Yeah, right," Lane heard a second voice answer the first, "filled with pictures of naked women."

"Joe, you are so full of shit it must be coming out your ears by now," the second voice continued in a tone of derision.

"Hey, I'm not making this shit up," the first voice said back, "I heard it on the radio."

Lane turned off the water and looked into the next stall, a towel tied around his waist.

It was empty.

He realized the acoustics of the bathroom had lied to his ears.

Scanning the bathroom he found the true source of the conversation. Two men stood at the row of sinks, shaving and talking. Their voices matched those he'd just heard.

"What about that car?" he asked them.

Both looked at Lane. The one who spoke up in answer was the one Lane had heard arguing that he'd heard about the Cadillac on the radio.

"So you heard about that too, huh?" he told

Lane. "Tell this guy it's the truth, willya pal? It was the car that killer in Amarillo was driving, wasn't it?"

"Sure," Lane said, his mind reeling. "Yeah, sure."

Bob was inside the room when Lane came back in. He stood at the window, looking out. The day was sunny and bright light streamed into the room.

"Hey, stranger," Bob called out cheerfully. "How 'bout this for a day? They sent a plow up to clear the pass last night and had some luck."

Bob turned and looked back out the window.

Lane stole a look at his pack, which sat on the bunk right next to Bob. The handle of the Colt was sticking out of the top. Had he left it that way when he'd gone out? Lane's eyes snapped back to the other man's face as Bob turned back to him.

"We got thirty minutes before the train leaves, pardner," he said, then stared hard at Lane and asked him if he was feeling all right. Lane was looking a mite green around the gills to him.

"I'm fine," Lane said. "Just a little tired."

"You sleep okay?"

"Yeah," Lane said.

"Thought for a minute there that maybe you

heard the police were lookin' for a car like mine," Bob went on, noticing the reaction in Lane's eyes. "A white Cadillac," he added unnecessarily.

"Yeah, I did in fact," Lane told him.

"Well, that car they're looking for had Texas plates," Bob elaborated, "mine had Oklahoma tags. Remember?"

Bob studied Lane's face.

"You believe me, don't ya, Doc?"

"Yeah. It just took me by surprise, that's all." Lane said.

Bob smiled broadly, looking relieved.

"Took *you* by surprise?" he declaimed. "How'd you think I felt when I heard about it?"

Bob picked up his coat and headed for the door. For a moment he stood between Lane and his gun.

"Well, I'm going downstairs to the TV and catch the weather," he said to Lane. "Throw your clothes on and we'll grab us a bite before we go."

Bob left, leaving Lane to stare at the closed door and then back at the handle of the Colt.

Bob sat in front of the TV set in the Eagle's ground floor parlor. He was watching the morning news alone as Lane came inside, his coat draped over his arm.

Lane closed the parlor door behind him and

watched Bob turn from the screen at the sound.

"See you're ready to roll, Doc," Bob said. "Great."

He got up and grabbed his own coat. Lane didn't budge from in front of the closed door.

"Where *did* you get that car?" he asked Bob in a quiet, level voice. Bob greeted his question with a laugh.

"Look, Doc, I can understand your concern, but you ever stop to think about how many white Caddies there probably are in the great state of Texas?"

"Probably a lot," Lane admitted.

"I'd say more than that," Bob told him.

Lane reached into the pocket of his coat and pulled out the revolver. He stood holding it against his thigh.

"But not that many with pictures," Lane added. "Where'd you get that car, Bob?"

Bob wasn't laughing anymore. He regarded Lane with a deadpan expression and brought his open hands out from his hips in the gesture of a man about to level with his questioner.

"Okay, pardner," he said. "I lied to you, I admit it. I wasn't taking the Caddy to no one. It's my car. Bought it in Tulsa only about four hours before I picked you up. But that don't mean I killed anyone."

Bob took a step toward Lane. The Colt was

pointing at his midsection before he could take a second.

"Stop right there," Lane ordered.

"I told you it was a friend's because I figured you'd feel too uncomfortable if you thought it was mine," Bob explained. "And wasn't I right? I was gonna throw all them pictures out when I got to Salt Lake."

He edged closer.

"They were a hoot, though, weren't they," he said, smiling again. "Those pictures sure were something."

Bob took another step and Lane thumbed back the Colt's hammer, cocking the firearm.

"Doc, listen to me!" Bob said, his voice rising. "If I was the killer, would I take you to all the places where I'm known? Introduce you to my friends? Hell, even save your neck?"

"I mean it," Lane said, not buying any of it. He tightened his finger on the trigger.

"Hell, if I was the killer why didn't I kill you?" Bob went on. "I had plenty of chances."

As he took one last step toward Lane, gesturing, Lane pulled the trigger.

The gun went off with a loud report and a bullet augered into the wall just behind Bob's head, sending out a plume of lathe and plaster. Bob raised his arm in a protective reflex as Lane cocked the pistol again.

"Goddammit! It was *my* car!" Bob shouted.

By now Al and a few other patrons had gathered in the hall and thrown open the door. Bob held a hand up. He wanted them to keep out of it.

"Prove it!" Lane shouted back at Bob.

"With what?" Bob countered. "I got off a train and bought it off a fella for five hundred bucks. I knew it wasn't on the up and up 'cause of the price."

Bob was pleading.

"What did you expect me to do, ask for a receipt?" He paused a beat and went on, "That's the truth, Doc. And if you can't trust me, then turn me in, 'cause all I got to back me up is my word."

The two men stared at each other. Lane was still pointing the Colt at Bob when they suddenly heard the local news anchor on the lounge TV. "Amarillo City police announced this morning that they are filing formal charges against a man suspected in the murder of three people there Saturday," she said.

Bob and Lane both looked simultaneously at the television screen where the video feed had cut to a shot of Jack McGinnis addressing a group of reporters at a police press conference.

"I want to thank the combined efforts of the city police and forensic departments for the arrest of this killer," McGinnis said, standing behind the podium. "The suspect's name is Hector Saldez. Mr. Saldez has been wanted in

New Mexico and Oklahoma on assault charges. Both of these states have waived extradition so that we may proceed with the prosecution."

A lady reporter stood up holding a ruled yellow legal pad. "Chief, do these murders have any connection to the Colorado murder last night?" she asked McGinnis.

"I can't comment on that investigation, Joyce," he told her.

Lane and Bob met each other's eyes again, and Lane lowered the gun.

They stood frozen for a long moment, and then Bob walked stiffly past Lane and out the door, saying nothing as he headed to the porch where Al was standing looking out onto the street.

"Just an accident, Al," he told the Eagle's proprietor, forcing himself to smile despite his anger. "Nothing to get all excited about. Let me know what we owe you for damages."

Without a backward glance, Bob walked down the street toward the train station.

18

The Colorado Highway Patrol vehicle was parked by the spot where Frank's car had broken through the snowbank. A state trooper checked for skid marks on the road and then followed the car's tracks down to the river. Frank's headlights, those that weren't submerged, glowed only dimly in the milky light of dawn. They had obviously been on long enough to severely deplete the battery.

The trooper watched his partner walk out onto the trestle and look through the ties at the icy swirling waters below. Every few steps he would lift his face into the stiff Colorado wind and peer up and down the tracks, just in case.

The trooper worked his way down the riverbank and under the bridge, trying to keep his footing while making sure not to miss anything. Thirty feet beyond the bridge, his diligence paid off. He spotted a sodden shoe wedged into some rocks at the water's edge.

Prying it free, he held the shoe aloft and yelled at his partner on the bridge. The second trooper was too far from the first for him to make out what he was saying.

But, then again, it was fairly obvious what his partner's discovery meant.

Olmstead moved quickly toward the bars of his cell in the Amarillo lockup, a stunned expression on his face.

"What?" he asked Nate who stood on the opposite side of the bars.

"Colorado HP found LaCrosse's car near a railroad trestle out of town," Nate told him. "They're searching the river now for his body. They believe he fell in while trying to board a train."

"A train?" Olmstead repeated.

"A Denver and Rio Grande freight," Nate confirmed. "The two-eighteen."

Olmstead grabbed the bars, his knuckles whitening with tension.

"Two-eighteen," he said in disbelief. "Then it wasn't a date. The son-of-a-bitch set Frank up! Nate, we've got to get in touch with that train."

"No can do," Nate said back. "It's out of contact till it gets to the other side. Storm's knocked out radio transmissions."

"When the hell's that?"

"Five hours."

Olmstead pounded the bars. "Damn!" he shouted. "The bastard knew Frank wouldn't give up, so he drew him in. He made us think we were all such goddamn great detectives, and the whole time he was leading Frank right to him."

"Are you saying the killer was expecting him to be there?"

"That's right," Olmstead affirmed with a nod. "And I helped deliver him."

Asleep in the caboose, LaCrosse did not realize that the train had stopped at a side track not far from La Veta, nor did he hear the steady crunch of boots in the packed snow beside the tracks, snow that had been plowed aside the night before.

It was only as the newcomer stepped atop the rear platform of the caboose that LaCrosse came awake and instantly drew his Sig from its shoulder holster. Moving quickly, LaCrosse flattened himself into a blind spot along the wall.

He watched the door open and close as the newcomer entered. He saw that it was a man dressed in a sheepskin coat, work-stained railroad cap, heavy gloves, and high lace-up work boots.

He waited until the man turned to light the oil stove near the door. Then he slipped from his hiding place and pressed the muzzle of the automatic against the side of the newcomer's head.

The man froze like a deer in a headlight.

"Who are you?" LaCrosse demanded.

"R-Ray Calabrese," he returned in a voice quaking with fear. "Don't shoot me, please!"

LaCrosse had put his gun away. He'd decided by now that the brakeman was a legitimate railway employee.

The two men sat at a small table in the drafty caboose with the oil stove doing what it could to dispel the severe chill.

Calabrese poured LaCrosse a cup of hot black coffee from a silver thermos. He eyed the Fed's shoeless right foot.

"How'd you loose your shoe?" he asked, now helping himself to a cup.

"Getting on this train," LaCrosse replied. "How'd you get here?"

"I was with the crew that cleared La Veta Pass last night," Calabrese answered. "Everyone else went back down to Martinsburg with the plow. I live in Salida, on the other side of the pass. The two-eighteen picks me up here and takes me home."

Just then the diesel's horn sounded.

The two-way communicator hanging from the brakeman's belt beeped two short high-low electronic tones. The engineer in the locomotive was signaling him that he was about to fire up the diesel and get moving.

"When's the next one due over?" Frank asked.

"This is it for the day."

"That's not possible." Frank all but stood up. "There's got to be another one."

"Not unless you want to climb the hill to the upper grade at Understanding and catch the Twenty-ten," Ray responded.

Frank put his coffee cup on the table and his face grew hard as he thought.

"There are two lines through the pass," Ray offered. "The upper grade is on the other side of the hill."

"What's Understanding? A town?"

Ray laughed at the serious way he asked. "No, a siding."

Ray pulled a railroad timetable from a hook on the wall and spread out the map of the rail line on the table. The sidings were listed like towns along a highway. Frank's finger traced a line from La Veta past Understanding to Believe. He tapped the last one harder and harder.

"When's it come through?" he finally said.

"The Twenty-ten? In about an hour."

Frank got up and went to the rear of the caboose, one shoe clumping on the floor.

"You can't go out there like that," Ray protested.

Frank opened the door and peered at the

sky. Then he practically growled, "Watch me."

Ray rushed forward, following Frank outside. As the agent leaned over the edge of the railing, readying himself to descend the boarding steps, Ray put a hand on his shoulder. "Wait."

When Ray removed his hand; Frank turned. He saw Ray bend down and unlace his insulated workboots.

The brakeman didn't feel like a fool, but he damned sure knew he looked like one as he stood at the railing of the caboose, watching LaCrosse pick his way along the track to the tunnel mouth.

Once he'd started giving away his boots, he realized he'd better give LaCrosse his gloves, too, and once he'd given him the gloves, he figured he'd need his sweater and heavy down coat.

Now Calabrese was dressed in a motley amalgam of Saville Row and Casey Jones, with LaCrosse's camel topcoat covering his pinstriped railway overalls, and one foot shod in a black wing-tip Oxford while the other was clothed only in a slightly sweaty wool sock.

As the caboose headed for the tunnel, Calabrese waved to LaCrosse, who had walked up the line, but the other man did not respond.

He was already beginning to climb the treacherously icy cliffside in an attempt to reach the top of the tunnel's mouth with enough time to spare to enable him to try boarding the next freight.

Lane walked down the stairs into the lobby of the Eagle Hotel. His coat was on and his pack was slung over his shoulder. He stopped at the front desk. Al stood behind it.

"What do I owe you?" he asked the manager.

"The bill's already been settled," he told Lane gruffly. "Bob's paid it."

Lane was surprised to hear that.

"Do you know where I could find him?" he asked.

"Over at the freight office," Al snapped, and looked away.

Lane started for the door, shouldering his pack.

"Lucky for you it was Bob you took that shot at," he heard Al holler after him. "If it had been me, I'd of killed you."

Lane stopped at the door, then returned to the front desk. He dropped his pack onto the counter and gingerly pulled out the gun he'd nearly killed Bob with. "Sorry," he said, setting it there.

For a moment he felt like a doctor again. He was meant to save people, not shoot them.

*　　*　　*

Lane found Bob sitting by a locker in the railway station's waiting room. He held a Styrofoam cup full of steaming black coffee in his hand.

A group of hard-looking men in work clothes and overalls eyed Lane as he came inside. Lane could tell that word of the shooting had gotten around La Veta.

"Can I talk to you?" he asked Bob.

The group of men each nodded at Bob and filed out of the station, leaving him and Lane alone.

"I'm sorry," Lane went on, although Bob hadn't answered. "I shouldn't have doubted you."

Bob sipped his coffee and reflected a moment on what Lane had said.

"Doc," he finally answered, "if I'd been in your shoes, hearing what you'd heard, I'd have probably held a gun on me too."

"If the offer's still open, I'm going over with you," Lane told him.

"Glad to have you, pardner," Bob said, and extended his hand. Lane grasped it and they shook.

A spreader car looks like the strangest of birds. Used to clear snow from the tracks, it has a high cupola and metal retractable "wings" tucked against its sides. Normally it led a locomotive through a pass, but this one had its claws firmly set in the end of a train, as if it had come in for the kill and was holding on until its prey submitted.

When Lane reached the spreader, he saw Bob standing on its rear platform with an old railroad man. They helped Lane aboard as the train lurched and moved out of the yard.

"Doc, this crusty old thing here is Tex Munroe," Bob said. "Tex, Doc Dixon."

"Welcome, welcome," Tex told Lane. "Any friend of this man is a friend of mine."

From inside his coat, Bob took out a pint of Irish whiskey. Tex's eyes lit up with pure joy when Bob handed the virgin bottle over to him. He slit the black bonding seal with his thumbnail and unscrewed the cap.

"Used to be you offered a man some coffee before you got to jawin', Tex," Bob told the veteran with a smile.

Tex bowed at that with the grace of a Vaudeville showman.

Straightening up, he pulled open the spreader's door and flourished his arm in a grand gesture of invitation. Bob and Lane went inside as the train headed for the pass and Tex followed, the pint of Irish in his hand.

Flanked by two of his people, Montgomery stood outside the cell in the Amarillo lockup, looking in at Buck.

Olmstead had been talking at him, but the Fed wasn't paying attention.

What they had here was called failure to communicate, went the old movie line in Olmstead's head. But the consequences could be fatal, Olmstead knew.

Frank was still alive. He could feel it in his bones. But he was up against hopeless odds with no backup.

"That man's life is on the line up there," he pleaded with Montgomery. "He's after a killer. He needs help!"

"A killer who's dead," Montgomery corrected, his expression bland and his voice noncommittal.

"No, dammit! He's not dead," Olmstead shouted. "If you won't help him, then at least let me out and I will."

"You've helped the FBI enough already, don't you think?" Montgomery countered acidly.

He eyed Olmstead, then turned to leave. The two other Feds whirled in lockstep and followed at their boss's heels.

"For God's sake, man!" Olmstead shouted after him, clutching the bars of the cell. "He's trying to find his son!"

Montgomery stopped and turned to look back at Olmstead.

The man was pathetic, he thought to himself.

He hadn't thought much of him from the beginning. But now he had truly plumbed the depths.

"It's a pipe dream, Sheriff," he told Olmstead dismissively. "Forget it."

The three men filed out of the lockup.

Only McGinnis remained behind.

Olmstead's arch rival said nothing as he paused for a moment. Then he too turned and wordlessly began to leave.

"Jack." Olmstead's voice was desperate.

McGinnis stopped and looked out the door, watching Montgomery and his two dark-suited brackets walk through the anteroom toward the elevators before he turned back toward the cells.

"I need some help here, Jack," Olmstead repeated.

Finally, after he saw the other men leave, McGinnis went back over to Olmstead's cell and spoke to him.

"I wish I could help you, Buck," he told him. "But the Feds have jurisdiction. By the time it would take me to get a hearing, it would all be history."

"A hearing's not what I need, Jack," Olmstead retorted. "What I need is for you to turn the key."

McGinnis tried to hold Olmstead's steady stare but couldn't.

"Christ, Buck," he answered, averting his

eyes, "this is the last thing I need today . . ." His voice trailed off.

"Yes it is," Olmstead countered.

McGinnis looked back at Olmstead, shook his head a couple of times, then, inhaling, looked aside at Robby, the jailer sitting at the end of the cell-block corridor.

Robby was watching him too, he realized.

"Open the door, Robby," he said finally, in a tone of resignation, still shaking his head as if he knew that it was a real dumb thing to do on the first day of his new job as Sheriff of Amarillo, Texas.

Robby had thrown the switch that opened Olmstead's cell door in a split second. He was grinning from ear to ear.

Buck stepped out and clapped McGinnis on the shoulder.

"You're off to a damn good start, Jack," he said with a laugh as Robby came over with Olmstead's coat and hat.

"Anything else you need?" McGinnis asked, not meaning it in the least by the look on his face and the rasp in his voice.

Olmstead was already shrugging on his coat as Robby fixed his hat on his head and handed him his gun belt.

"Now that you mention it, Jack," he told McGinnis, "there is."

19

With a last grunt of effort, Frank cleared the top of the hill. Encrusted with frozen meltwater and snow, the slope had offered little secure footing, and Frank had nearly fallen to his death on more than one occasion while ascending.

Now the mouth of a tunnel that enabled the other line to cross the pass lay far below him at the bottom of a rocky, ice-patched cliff. It hadn't promised much in the way of handholds. Frank took a moment to catch his breath and remember what stable ground is like to stand on. Then he slowly started down.

On just his third step, he dislodged a cascade of snow and stone that crashed down over the tunnel mouth.

Frank paused again to consider the fall more fully.

"Getting close to the pass," Tex said to his guests aboard the spreader, checking his pocket watch. He proceeded to refill his briar pipe. The second bowlful of tobacco would taste even smoother now that he had drunk most of the bottle of Irish.

"They've lost whole trains in avalanches up here," Tex went on as he tamped the tobacco into the bowl. "Not found them till months later."

The old railway man looked over at Lane, who sat in the cupola gazing out over the rugged, snow-covered landscape that fell away into steep-sided ravines as the train climbed higher into the mountains. He absently ran his hand over a control lever.

Bob sat on an upended crate, whittling on a block of wood. Shavings lay scattered around Bob's scuffed and snow-stained cowboy boots. He looked up and saw what Lane was doing at the same Tex did.

"Careful what you touch up there," Bob warned him.

"Yessir," Tex said, "those levers control them four-ton wings out there. You send one out by accident and we might have a little trouble getting through the next tunnel."

Tex and Bob chuckled like two veteran ballplayers amused by a rookie's error.

Tex, now that his pipe was lit, got out the bottle of Irish again and poured a little more of the golden fluid into a porcelain drinking cup. Lane noticed that not too much was left of the virgin bottle anymore.

After Tex took a sip, Lane asked, "What controls the wings?"

"Them big air tanks in the main compartment. You can operate them up where you're sitting, by the tanks, or off the back platform where we got on."

Lane secretly touched the control lever again. He never liked being the rook. "Is working this thing your job?"

"Me?" Tex responded. "No, I'm just hauling this spreader over to Salida. Clearing passes is a job I never cottoned-to. Night work, mostly. And cold." He took another pull on his pipe. "Bobby used to clear these passes up here, though."

"So I heard."

Bob stopped his whittling, took out a small whetstone, and began sharpening his knife with slow, even strokes as he watched Tex smile and knock back the Irish.

"That was a long time ago," Bob told him, and started back on the whetstone, honing the knife edge to razor-sharpness.

Fifty feet above the tunnel mouth, LaCrosse teetered precariously across the ice-slicked rock ledge.

The muscles in his arms, legs, and back ached from the punishing descent; and the cold was so intense that even with the clothes Calabrese had given him it had taken its toll.

His body was wracked with shivers and his breathing was stertorous as he rubbed his hands together and blew into them in a vain effort to warm the numbed, frostbitten fingers.

Yet LaCrosse knew that he would have to move again soon and somehow muster the strength to accomplish what he must do next. In the distance, the faint rumbling that he had heard midway to the summit had since become the deep, throbbing tumult of the approaching freight's diesel engines.

The sound grew louder, and soon the ground beneath LaCrosse's feet began to shake. In a moment he saw the first locomotive suddenly top La Veta pass, picking up speed as it took the straightaway toward the tunnel.

Summoning his last reserves of strength, LaCrosse began climbing down from the rock ledge, toward the lip of the railway tunnel below. Hurrying to meet the train, his hands missed a grip and he began tumbling down the steep, ice-encrusted incline between the ledge and the tunnel, crashing through snow and rocks as the train plunged headlong down the track, straight for the tunnel mouth.

Though he clawed desperately, trying to grasp anything that might arrest his fall, LaCrosse continued to skid down the slope until he came to the rough-hewn stone coping at the lip of the tunnel. Here he managed to gain a handhold as his entire body swung precariously over the edge.

In the space of an eye-blink, the first locomotive darted from the yawning cavern, a blue bullet against the dazzling white snow. LaCrosse struggled to pull himself up as the train passed beneath him.

He wasn't ready yet.

Tex's pipe had gone out again and he'd run out of matches.

"Anybody got a light?" he asked, patting his shirt pockets.

Lane shook his head, but Bob absently reached into his jacket and took out a book of matches, which he handed to Tex.

With a thankful nod Bob's way, Tex lit up his pipe, then suddenly gave a start.

"Well, I'll be damned," he said, holding up the matchbook to show it to Bob. "This here's the place where them murders were in Amarillo."

Lane turned from the window at this remark as Tex continued to contemplate the matchbook Bob had just given him.

"Yup. Same motel in Amarillo," he said with a nod. "Been on the news for two days runnin'."

The old-timer looked up, noticing that his

guests were staring at each other in a funny kind of way.

He could instantly feel the tension. It was so thick you could cut it with a knife.

"Did I just say something?" Tex asked lamely, looking from Lane to Bob and back again.

"Yeah, Tex," Bob answered, "you sure did."

The roar of the passing freight was deafening. Waves of compressed air thrown up as the train sped into the tunnel mouth buffeted LaCrosse, threatening to dislodge his already precarious handhold on the slabs of rock coping that lined the tunnel mouth.

Powdery snow swirled around his head, blinding him as he struggled to pull himself above the tunnel entrance. His already strained and punished muscles performed despite the spasms of fatigue and waves of vertigo that were setting in. He chanced a glance down and saw the immense black hoppers full of bituminous coal speed by on the dozens of hitched flatcars. A chunk of ice-encrusted rock fell past him and was crushed to powder beneath the train's merciless steel wheels—just as he knew he would be if he didn't time things perfectly. He turned his head away and concentrated on doing the impossible.

The plan he had formulated as he hiked from the other train depended entirely on a single difficult maneuver. He had to drop into one of the open coal hoppers and hope the snow broke his fall. He had counted on being able to get this close. What he hadn't counted on were the hot needles of exhaustion that lanced through his arms and indicated they would give out any second.

"Well, I hope I didn't say nothin' bad," Tex said as Bob took his whetstone back out and sharpened his knife some more.

"Nothing bad, Tex," Bob told the veteran. "It's just ol' Doc over there's got me pegged as a killer right about now."

Tex looked at Lane as though he were insane. Bob kept sliding the blade along the whetstone using even, forward strokes.

"Now where in Sam Hill did you get a crazy notion like that?" he demanded of Lane. "They're lookin' for a young fella. Light brown hair. Sorta like yours, in fact," Tex added insinuatingly.

Motioning at Bob with the stem of his briar pipe, Tex patted his old buddy on the back with his free hand.

"This man here," Tex began, "why he's the salt of the earth. Salt of the gol' danged—"

The old man's words were stopped short as Bob put the knife inside him, effortlessly sliding the razor-sharp point of the knife into Tex's inner thigh, just below the groin.

Tex's eyes went wide as saucers. The pipe and matchbook slipped from his hands. The knife was now buried up to the hilt.

Tex's spurting arterial blood began to spread down his pants legs. A dark, wet blotch grew as more blood poured out and onto the floor between his legs.

Lane was on his feet, lurching forward to help the stricken man, but Bob had pulled the knife out by then and now pointed its incarnadined blade at Lane.

"Sit down, Doc," he ordered.

"Christ! Let me help him!" Lane pleaded.

"Too late, Doc," Bob said. "Ain't nothing you can do."

Tex was blubbering in pain and terror as he held his hands over his wounded groin, but the blood kept gushing out through his fingers despite everything he did to stop it.

Bob looked him over without a trace of emotion. The look of viciousness that came over his face a moment later he reserved for Lane, turning to him.

The moment when LaCrosse's fingers lost their ability to hold on to the rock came with terrible suddenness.

One moment LaCrosse was holding on, the next he wasn't.

It wasn't even a matter of willpower anymore.

His hands were now no longer a part of him.

They were dead things.

And now, so was he.

LaCrosse felt himself drop from the arched top of the tunnel mouth and go into free fall.

Darkness immediately swallowed him as he fell backward, his arms and legs splayed outward by the overpressure caused by the train speeding through the tunnel.

A second later he felt his spine strike something hard.

And then the darkness was complete.

Lane bent down and picked the matchbook up off the floor from where Tex had dropped it.

Printed on its cover he read the words: Tall Indian Restaurant.

"You followed me from the motel," he said, looking at Bob. He could imagine it all, just as it had probably happened.

Lane saw himself leave Room 103 and come down the motel's stairs.

"I had a nice seat at the restaurant the next morning when you came down for breakfast," Bob told him, confirming his suspicion.

Lane saw himself taking a seat next to the rancher and his young daughter.

Bob nodded as if reading his mind. Lane

was right. It had gone down pretty much like the way he'd guessed.

"I heard you ask for a ride," Bob affirmed, and Lane's memory played back the rancher's words as the man had asked him how far he was going. Lane next recalled how the rancher's pickup had left the restaurant. Bob had probably been watching all along.

"Then I paid your friend, Mr. Suderland, a little visit," Bob said, replaying the chain of events that led him to the killing.

He saw Suderland naked in the shower.

He saw himself entering the room, moving like a ghost toward the sound of the running water, the knife clutched in his hand.

He saw his victim come into view.

Saw himself raise the knife, slide it inside, and cut deep into his flesh—and the dark hot blood begin to spurt into the steam and the running water.

Lane was looking at Bob as if Bob were the most despicable thing on the face of the earth.

Suderland, a total stranger, had given him a ride, befriended him, loaned him money he'd never expected to get back, let him share his motel room. And Bob had rewarded his kindness with death.

"They'll find you," was all Lane managed to say.

"I don't think so," Bob replied. "Like Tex said, they ain't looking for me. They're looking for you." Bob gestured with the knife toward Lane's pack. "Pass me your pack now. I need that gun."

Lane had no choice. He slid the pack over to Bob. But his eye had strayed to something propped against the wall in a corner.

A shovel.

It was the unnaturally high air pressure caused by the train that had saved his life, LaCrosse realized. It had cushioned his fall. That and the fact that he had landed on a bed of soft chunks of coal instead of something much harder, such as the unforgiving steel roof of a boxcar.

Scrambling to his feet, LaCrosse grasped the side of the coal hopper and raised himself to peer over the edge.

Luck was with him, at least after a fashion.

The train's caboose was just behind the hopper. With a queasy feeling in his gut, he realized that if he had fallen a second later, the outcome would have been far different.

Just the same, there was a joker in the deck.

A wide gap of maybe five feet separated the rear of the coal hopper from the railing at the front of the caboose.

LaCrosse knew that he'd have to jump it.

20

Bob had opened Lane's backpack and was looking inside it for the Colt. For only a moment or two he had turned his head away, but Lane saw his chance and took it.

As Bob looked up, wondering where it could be, Lane lunged for the shovel and brought it to bear on Bob's temple. Bob only had enough time to raise a hand in a reflexive gesture, worthless against what was coming at him.

The shovel crashed into the side of Bob's skull with a loud, hollow thunk. Lane felt the shock of the impact travel up his arms and into his shoulders.

If a shovel had a sweet spot, somehow Lane had found it.

Inside Bob's head, somebody had lit a blowtorch.

The pain seared him; the light blinded him.

Then, just as suddenly, the blowtorch was extinguished, leaving oblivion in its wake.

Lane looked down at Bob, who was now sprawled on the bloodstained floor of the caboose. His knife was lying right beside him.

There was a slight gash in the side of Bob's head where the shovel had struck him, but now Lane didn't feel like playing doctor.

Instead he bent down and reached for the knife.

LaCrosse took several deep breaths and tensed his muscles for the jump across the gap between the caboose and the coal car on which he rode. He mentally counted down from three and swung his arms forward to put all his body mass into the jump.

A heartbeat later, he was leaping across five feet of empty space, surprised to find that he had actually made it successfully and the wooden decking of the front platform of the caboose was under the soles of his boots.

An instant later LaCrosse drew his Sig from its shoulder holster and kicked open the front door of the caboose.

With the Sig held in a two-handed combat grip, he crabbed inside in a half-crouch, his eyes scanning the interior for any sign of threat.

Adrenaline fed LaCrosse's situational awareness. In a fleeting instant, his brain processed the information that his eyes and the rest of his senses were feeding him.

A brown-haired man of the approximate age and description of the serial killer was crouched over another, older man slumped on the floor and covered with blood. Near the door a third man lay prone on the caboose's swaying deck, apparently unconscious, possibly dead.

In the second before he acted, LaCrosse drew a set of conclusions from the scene. Conclusions which, though inescapable, happened to be entirely wrong.

"Freeze!" he shouted, pointing the gun at Lane.

Lane turned toward the source of the shout and saw LaCrosse standing in the open front door of the caboose.

He didn't know who he was or how he'd gotten aboard, but none of that mattered at the moment. The fact that there was a gun being pointed at him, that was the bottom line.

"*He* killed him," Lane tried to explain, seeing the mute accusation in the other man's eyes. "He was going to kill me."

Then LaCrosse saw Bob's knife lying at Lane's feet. It was exactly the type of knife the killer had probably used.

It only reconfirmed the false suppositions LaCrosse had made under stress and in the heat of the moment. LaCrosse wasn't buying Lane's story.

The way he called it, he'd just found his man.

"Move the knife aside and get away from him," he ordered Lane.

At that moment Lane flashed on what must be going through the newcomer's mind. He must know about the murders, Lane told himself. He might be a cop. And he thinks I'm the one who did the crimes.

"I didn't kill him," Lane said again, trying to reason with his accuser.

"Move the knife away!"

LaCrosse was shouting his order this time.

It was apparent to Lane that he was on the edge of fatal violence, incapable of seeing things as they truly were.

Lane had no choice now. He kicked away the knife with the side of his boot.

LaCrosse was on top of him in a second, shoving him up against the wall of the caboose.

"Where is he?" LaCrosse demanded, bunching his shirt collar in one hand.

"What?"

Lane saw madness in his attacker's eyes, an unreasoning hatred of him that would permit no explanation other than the one his assailant expected.

Lane had no doubt that he was in mortal danger.

"Don't fuck with me," LaCrosse snarled. "I *will* kill you to find him."

Locked in their struggle, neither man saw what was happening on the floor near the front of the caboose.

They did not see Bob open his eyes and sit up as consciousness returned. Nor did they see him spot the bowie knife lying near him and stretch a hand toward it.

LaCrosse cocked the hammer of the Sig. He would show Lane that he meant what he had said.

In that instant he heard the rustle of movement behind him and saw Lane's eyes widen as they looked past his face.

"Watch out!" Lane shouted.

LaCrosse turned and saw Bob coming at him with the blade held low in a classic knife-fighter's grip.

He brought up his gun hand and tried to draw a bead as his assailant lurched toward him, sweeping the knife out from the center of his body in a series of glittering arcs, but he couldn't react quickly enough.

Before LaCrosse could get off a round, Bob thrust at him, cutting through his coat sleeve and slashing deep into his arm.

And to make matters worse, at that moment the train drove into another of the many tunnels in the pass, plunging the spreader into darkness.

LaCrosse suddenly lost the ability to grip, and the gun fell from his hand. He heard it go skidding across the juddering deck of the spreader as Bob slashed at him again, wildly slicing through muscle and tendons and opening LaCrosse's veins as easily as paper straws. Slipping on a patch of his own slick blood, he went crashing against a metal locker bolted to the wall of the caboose.

Huddled near the cabinet in pitch darkness as the train negotiated the tunnel, LaCrosse held out his arms to block any more strikes from Bob. But none came, and then the caboose was out in daylight again.

He saw the dull steel of his weapon lying only a few feet away.

In another second he had the Sig in his hands and was bringing it up to sight on Bob.

But by this time Bob had also reacted to the light's return.

To his chagrin, LaCrosse saw that he now held Lane in front of him, a human shield. Bob's arm was curled tight around Lane's neck, making him gurgle as he tried to speak. Bob intended the coming conversation to be two-way only.

"You made good time, Frank," Bob told LaCrosse. "I have to admit I was worried for a while that you'd make it at all. Drop the gun so we can talk civilized."

LaCrosse shook his head and held on to the

Sig. Smiling, Bob jerked Lane's head back, tightening his grip. Lane's back arched, trying to find some relief.

"I'll cut his throat if you don't drop that pistol, Frank," Bob threatened, bringing the wickedly honed edge of the knife to the exposed part of Lane's throat under his arm.

"It won't work," LaCrosse told him. "State police know you're on this train. They know I'm on it. They'll be waiting for you the minute we're over the mountains."

"Always needing help, aren't you Frank?" Bob retorted. "You didn't start out that way. In the beginning, when it was just me and you, it was a challenge. I made a move, then you made a move." He tapped the knife edge to the left then the right of Lane's throat. "But then you had to start playing the game unfairly."

"Never was a game."

"Oh yes it was. Me against you. Then it was me against you and fifty other agents. Then two hundred agents." Realizing that Frank probably wasn't bluffing about the state police, Bob began to edge slowly toward the rear of the car, his back to the wall, Lane right in front of him. The knife never left Lane's throat.

Frank's aim followed him, barely wavering from a near impossible headshot. "You didn't seem to be having any trouble," he said over the gun.

"Don't bullshit me, Frank. It wasn't fair. I had to level the playing field." He paused and got a better grip on Lane. "That's why I took your boy."

Lane's eyes, which had been darting left and right loooking for some way to get loose, suddenly froze on Frank. He hoped Frank would notice.

Frank only focused on Bob, though. "Where is he?"

"Remember the deal," Bob hissed. " 'Kill me to find him.' "

Lane tried to lower his head to whisper something with what air Bob allowed him, but Bob glared at him and stopped his words by cutting slowly into the outer skin of his neck. Lane involuntarily held his breath as Bob drew a thin red line with the keen tip of his blade toward Lane's carotid artery.

Frank tried to maneuver around the spreader for a better shot, but Bob kept Lane between them and never exposed his back. He moved closer to the rear door. Blood started to trickle slowly down Lane's neck and chest. Bob began to laugh at their dance as Frank darted more sharply to draw a bead, but he knew it was no use.

If he wanted Bob, he would have to take down Lane.

LaCrosse's finger tensed on the Sig's trigger. So close, he thought. So easy.

All he had to do was squeeze the trigger a fraction of an inch, squeeze it past the break-point, and it would all be over, the nightmare would end.

But he couldn't. Worse, Bob knew he couldn't.

Lane considered the head shot again. Under shooting range conditions, LaCrosse estimated he'd have maybe a fifty-fifty chance of making it, even with luck on his side.

But he wasn't on the range now.

He was standing on the swaying deck of the last car of a hurtling freight train that could, like the rattles on a diamondback's tail, whip around at any moment if the train took a sudden turn, and make the shot go wild.

LaCrosse's eyes fixed on the tip of the knife. It was now a fraction of an inch from the bulging carotid artery on Lane's neck. Still, he continued to hold his fire.

There was another option, he realized. A horrible one.

"You're really thinking about letting me kill him, aren't you Frank," Bob said as if reading his thoughts. "Have you become that cold?"

The banshee wail of the train's diesel horn suddenly cut through the tense silence between the two antagonists.

The engineer was sounding it to warn of the approach of a new tunnel, one with no clearance for anyone leaning their head out from the protection of the cars.

To Bob's trained ear the noise was the sound of salvation itself.

In the darkness that would soon come, LaCrosse would be unable to aim. His chances of hitting him would be reduced practically to zero.

The odds, Bob knew, were tilting in his favor.

He'd escape to kill again.

Bob pulled Lane the rest of the way to the rear door of the spreader. Reaching behind him, he turned the knob and threw it open, still managing to keep Lane securely in front of him.

A wider trickle of blood slipped down Lane's neck. Lane stiffened, but Bob didn't notice it wasn't out of fear now, but realization. And resolve.

"You had your chance, Frank," Bob told LaCrosse as he stood framed in the open doorway, blue sky behind his head. "You should have taken it."

Lane locked his eyes on to Frank's. Frank's gun remained locked on Bob.

In the last second before the darkness engulfed them, Bob grinned.

"Good-bye, Frank," he said and got ready to jump. He would take Lane with him and finish him off if the fall didn't kill him.

That's when Lane made his move.

He jerked his head sideways, drawing his neck across the blade, but giving Frank the clean shot he'd been hoping for.

The apparently suicidal maneuver took Bob completely by surprise. He'd only begun to realize what it meant for him when from far away, it seemed, he heard an explosion.

LaCrosse had squeezed off a parabellum round and saw Bob's right cheek vaporize in a mist of blood and bone.

He'd scored.

Skewed half around by the bullet's impact, Bob let go of Lane and went sprawling through the open door of the caboose, onto the rear platform beyond it. The diesel horn blared once more and the blackness of the tunnel completely wrapped itself around the car.

Feeling for Lane in the dark, LaCrosse pulled a handkerchief from his pocket when he found him and held it against the gash in Lane's neck.

Lane was trying to say something to La-Crosse but bubbles of blood foamed on his lips as he spoke and gurgled in his throat.

"Don't talk," LaCrosse told him, feeling guilty for this having happened. If he hadn't held on to his gun . . . but he couldn't dwell on that now. There was no point.

He took off his coat and covered the young

man. Then LaCrosse saw Lane's eyes dart toward the doorway behind them.

He pivoted quickly, bringing up his gun, but the doorway was empty. The rear platform too appeared deserted as LaCrosse peered through the door. LaCrosse put the gun back down and tied the handkerchief around Lane's throat.

Just paranoia, he thought. Bob was history.

Or was he?

Lane tried speaking to him again, and LaCrosse knew he desperately wanted to tell him something. But he was too weak to talk now, and Lane finally gave up. LaCrosse covered Lane with his coat as he closed his eyes and lay on the floor trying to marshal his strength.

"Rest," LaCrosse told him. "We'll talk later."

A jarring sound, like something metallic banging against the platform railing, suddenly broke through the steady, rhythmic clattering of the train's passage across the tracks.

"I'll be back," LaCrosse told Lane.

Taking up his gun again, LaCrosse moved along the wall toward the frame of the open door. The even-paced metallic clanging continued. His body flat against the wall, he risked a quick peek outside.

Nothing.

Sky, mountains, track, snow.

Nothing else.

But the clanging noise still grated against his ears, and LaCrosse realized he'd have to go outside in order to determine what was causing it. Taking a deep breath and steadying himself, he stepped quickly from the caboose, fanning the Sig across the platform.

It was empty.

There was no trace of Bob.

The noise, LaCrosse quickly saw, was being caused by a loose length of chain from the rear hitch that depended from the rear of the caboose.

He untangled it, let it fall to the track bed, and watched it grow to a faint dark speck as the train left it behind.

It was over, he suddenly realized.

God, it was finally over.

Later, he knew, emotion would come flooding over him like waters breaking across a dam.

But that was still in the future.

Right now LaCrosse was too numb to feel anything but a sudden release from tension, an emptiness inside him where his guts had been tightened up in knots for far too long.

Totally drained, he simply stood on the platform, battered by the cold wind. He looked out across the valley below the trackway and recognized what he thought must be the town of La Veta far off in the distance.

LaCrosse continued to watch, until the train rounded a bend in the tracks and went behind the spur of a mountain and the view disappeared.

LaCrosse became aware of the gun in his hand, the heaviness of it as it dangled, leaden and useless, at his side. He wouldn't be needing it anymore. LaCrosse decocked the hammer and turned to go back inside the caboose.

Something darted from the side of the car.

A red blur, and then the cold glint of sunlight glancing off burnished steel as the long, sharp blade was thrust into his flesh.

LaCrosse grunted in pain.

Bob had swung from the roof onto the platform, the knife stabbing and slashing, the right side of his face a mass of dripping red gore.

LaCrosse tried to raise the Sig into position for a head shot, but Bob had the initiative. The knife lunged again, and blood spurted from LaCrosse's hand, the gun tumbling to the deck and slithering over the side.

Lost.

Again the knife came sweeping in, this time lashing out at LaCrosse's throat in a death swipe calculated to sever his windpipe and cut through his neck vertebrae.

LaCrosse managed to sidestep the reckless lunge, grabbing Bob's now overextended hand.

Locked together in a contest of brute physical strength, both men went tumbling through the open doorway and back into the interior of the spreader, where they crashed into the side of a stove.

LaCrosse's head struck it sharply. Stunned by the blow, he momentarily let go of Bob's knife hand and fell to the floor.

The instant was enough for Bob.

He coiled himself up inside like a cobra preparing to strike, then fell upon LaCrosse's helpless body. Before he could bring the knife across the femoral artery, though, he heard the radio crackle. Looking up, he saw Lane in the cupola, triggering the controls.

Bob grinned and turned his sights on Lane instead.

"You've got some nerve, Doc, interrupting my fun. But now it's time to give it up."

Lane watched Bob close in on him, staring him down. Then without moving his eyes, he yanked down on the air controls. A jet of compressed air from the spreader's tanks smashed into Bob's face.

Bob swam backward as if caught in a riptide. Across the car he regrouped, glanced at his knife, and charged at Lane. Bob barreled him forward into the corner, trapping him. The kill, Bob calculated, would be quick and efficient. He was sick of toying with Lane.

Lane did the only thing he could. He braced himself and watched it come.

But Bob hadn't figured Frank into the equation. Just as he was about to slide the knife home, Frank grabbed him from behind and wrestled him away. The two spun across the rocking car, a blur of muscle and sweat and steel, until their momentum flung them out the now open side of the spreader.

Lane's tactic had swung the wing away from the side of the spreader out into the snow.

Frank now had an even worse blade to contend with.

The fall outside had split Bob and him apart. Out of control, Frank had slid past the arm that held the wing in place to the bottom of the wing, where he came to rest inches from the edge. He pulled himself away, but only had time for a single breath of relief. Out of the corner of his eye he saw something that made his body fling itself down tight against the wing before he could even register what it was.

The wing tore through a massive drift and heaved a wall of snow back over the wing. Ice cut Frank's face. Then with a jarring crunch, wood chips and branches that once were a few small trees soon followed, rubbing splinters into the wounds.

Out here, with little to hold on to, he realized he could be brushed off the wing as easily as a bug off someone's arm.

Frank took a quick glance around to see where Bob was. Bob, it seemed, had also realized their predicament. He too had flattened himself against the wing higher up toward the spreader.

After a moment, Frank looked up over the wing to see if all would be clear for a moment so he could get the drop on Bob. To his horror the mountains, the tracks, and the train seemed suddenly gone. They'd been replaced by the onrushing wall of a signal shack.

The wing, made of four tons of indomitable metal, hacked through the shack like an ax through maple. Planks, shingles, posts, what might have been furniture, exploded over the wing. Frank was pelted with debris and lost his grip, dropping farther down the wing until his legs slipped over the edge.

He tried to push off the snow, but then the snow was gone, dropping away into a deep river gorge.

And Bob realized the advantage was his.

Working his way over the rattling wing, Bob sneered down at Frank, enjoying his struggle. Then he began to slam his bootheel down on Frank's hands.

Every time Frank's hand jerked free from the pain, Bob laughed and waited till it found a hold again. Then he smashed the other hand.

Bob was not sick of toying with Frank.

"Had enough, Frank?" he yelled.

Frank only gritted his teeth and ignored his bloody knuckles. His legs paddled madly at the air.

Bob's face dimmed and he smashed Frank's right hand again. This time, though, he began to grind his boot into the left one as well. The game was over.

Frank tried to drive the fingertips of his left hand through the metal wing, but it was useless. He could barely feel his fingers at all.

He knew he was going to fall.

He once told his wife not long after the birth of their son that if there were a perfect way to leave this earth, it would not be in the course of closing some grand investigation. It would not be while saving someone's life. He never wanted to be a hero or a martyr. All he wanted to be was a father. So the perfect place to die would be at home, in bed, with his son looking on. His son would know he loved him. Frank would know he wasn't really dying at all. And the last thing he would see would be his boy's face.

The final card fate had dealt him, though, was a face card with Bob's vicious, torn sneer.

Then fate dropped an ace in his lap.

For a moment the ground returned like a hand and boosted Frank's flailing legs roughly up onto the wing. Thrown forward, Frank crashed into Bob, sending him sliding wildly across the wing.

He disappeared over the edge just as the wing soared over another gorge.

"No!" Frank screamed, and scuttled over to the point where Bob had fallen.

But Bob hadn't. His hand had clenched into an iron grip on the edge.

Laying flat out on the wing, Frank reached over the edge and grabbed Bob's wrist.

Bob looked up and they locked eyes.

"Where is he?" Frank yelled over the roaring wind.

" 'Kill me to find him, Frank,' " he laughed. "That was our deal."

Bob let go of his grip and their hands slid down together. Frank clenched as hard as he could, but Bob twisted his arm as if to enjoy the panoramic view and managed to let go.

Frank watched as Bob bounced off the snow-packed side of the gorge and somersaulted backward down toward the bank of the river below. With each bounce he slowed, leaning forward into the hill, until it seemed he was running backward, then just backpedaling, then on the verge of being able to stop and stand.

Frank needed him alive. If Bob lived, he knew he would find him again. Bob would let him.

But that Bob might survive the fall tore at him, too.

As Bob's momentum carried him closer to

the water's edge he looked up at the wing.
Frank couldn't see his expression.

He only saw him smash a second later into
a tree and jerk wildly as a sharp branch, sil-
houetted against the snow, caught Bob in the
center of his back. The way he came to rest,
hanging limply against the tree, Frank knew
he was dead.

And so were his chances of finding his son.

Frank watched the ravine and Bob disappear behind him.

How would he start his search again?
Where would he begin? Dropping his head to
the wing, Frank wondered what his next move
would be.

The train's horn changed pitch and made
the decision for him. Frank looked back over
the wing and saw a tunnel bearing down on
the train. Only there was no way the wing was
going to make it through.

Frank tried to crawl up the wing, but his
hands were too bloody now to get a grip on
the tiny handholds it offered. His wounded
legs had stiffened and offered little help.

The wing took out another tree. Its broken
body shot past Frank like a warning.

Frank spotted the arm that held the wing in
place. He struggled to his knees and, lifting
himself, tried to fall forward at it, just grabbing the joint where it met the wing. Able to
get a firm grip, he climbed up hand over hand.

The open side of the spreader was only a few feet away.

The tunnel, five hundred feet away now and rapidly advancing, looked closer.

The cold edge of the metal arm bit into his hands as he climbed. It felt like he was shimmying up a sword. And his bloody legs felt like dead weight.

As he closed on the car, Frank noticed a thin chain dangling from the arm. Grabbing it, he leaped before his legs could realize they had no more energy to leap, and swung himself forward in one last desperate attempt to survive and find his son.

The roar of the train diving into the tunnel rushed back over Frank. He heard the mountain explode against the wing, ripping the four tons of metal off the spreader with a horrible shriek of metal on stone. He was bathed in a shower of sparks.

This is the sound of my death, he thought.

21

One of the two engineers in the cabin had his hand on the throttle. The other engineer was reading a newspaper. Suddenly the driver looked up through the window. Something had just glinted in the sunlight overhead.

In a moment, the police helicopter emblazoned with the shield of the Amarillo City Police appeared overhead. The chopper had matched its speed with that of the train and was pacing it about thirty feet above the lead locomotive.

The driver raised his work-gloved hand and waved at the chopper. Now what in the name of hell were the police doing here, he wondered?

Less than fifteen minutes later, the freight train sat on the tracks of a spur line in the valley, the police helicopter parked a short distance away on level ground. In the middle distance stood the western flank of the snow-capped Sangre de Cristo range.

Soon after seeing the chopper, the engineer's handheld radio had crackled with instructions to stop the train at the nearest possible location. The train was then to be boarded by law-enforcement personnel.

Two men walked toward the rear of the multicar freight express. One of them was the engineer who had spotted the chopper. The other man was Buck Olmstead.

"Well, Tex is an old fella," the engineer said, "but just 'cause he doesn't answer his radio don't mean—" He froze. "Sweet Jesus," he whispered, as Buck followed his look.

The wing dangled broken and bent from the side of the spreader, the twisted arm having a death grip on it. Its passage through the tunnel had also torn great rents in the side of the car.

Buck broke into a run, and the engineer signaled back to the locomotive where two Colorado State Patrol troopers stood with the other engineer.

Buck nearly threw himself through the rear door of the spreader. He saw Lane propped at the far end of the car and covered by Frank's coat. As he started toward him, he heard a muffled cough behind him, then, weakly:

"Buck."

He lay shivering in the corner, his cut leg crudely bandaged with a dirty rag.

"Oh, my God. Frank."

As Buck kneeled beside him and covered

Frank with his coat, the two troopers ran in. They immediately began to tend to Lane.

"I killed him, Buck," he told Olmstead.

"And your boy?" Olmstead said after a pause. It was a question he didn't want to ask.

LaCrosse shook his head. Olmstead was saddened, though not very surprised.

"Hang on," he told LaCrosse, there being nothing else he could say at this point. "We'll get you to a hospital."

One of the troopers was bandaging Lane's wounded neck, the other was looking over the interior.

"Don't talk," the first trooper said to Lane, who had been trying to tell him something in a voice too weak and guttural to be understood. "It'll be all right. We'll get you out of here."

The trooper surmised that Lane had been asking about his survival chances. He wanted to assure him that he would soon receive emergency medical care.

"He's lost a lot of blood, got hypothermia," he said to the other trooper, who nodded and made a notation on a spiral pad he'd taken from his pocket.

The first trooper suddenly felt something at his chest and looked down.

He saw that Lane had grabbed the pen from his breast pocket.

As he watched, dumbfounded, Lane began scrawling something on the floor of the spreader.

Olmstead was helping LaCrosse out of the spreader, when the second trooper called after him.

"Sir? You'd better come here fast."

Frank hobbled back to Lane.

"He's writing something," the trooper told him.

Crossing to Lane's side, LaCrosse crouched down and stared at the marks on the floor. What Lane was trying to tell him was almost beyond belief.

"Your son," Lane was writing. "I know."

The small East Bay house sat on a decaying street in Oakland, California, just across the bay from San Francisco. The windows and door of the house were boarded up and weeds grew thick in its front yard.

Over the door, in faded blue paint, were the numerals 8899.

LaCrosse stood in front of the house, leaning on a cane. He stared at the numbers. No words could describe the crushing sense of failure and depression that gripped him at that moment.

After all he'd been through, after all he had suffered, he had come to another dead end.

He continued staring at the sign, lost in his

own world, oblivious to the conversation in Spanish that Olmstead was holding nearby with one of the residents of the mostly Mexican block.

"He told me the city condemned it two months ago," Olmstead told LaCrosse when he was through. "Nobody's been there for months."

LaCrosse said nothing, didn't even nod.

He merely wandered off, limping slowly across the yard while Olmstead and the other man watched.

Reaching the front door, LaCrosse pried loose a board over the nearest window.

Through broken plate-glass he peered inside.

Soon he was working at the boards at the door, prying them loose in a fury.

He wanted to get inside.

Olmstead didn't try to stop him. He knew the man had to exorcise his demons. He waited until LaCrosse went through the door. Then he followed him in.

As the dust thrown up by their entrance settled, Buck saw the frame of light coming through the back door first, then the hallway, then the empty chair. It was the scene from Frank's photograph.

Buck tried to put a hand on Frank's shoulder, but Frank had already stumbled forward, moving toward the light as if drawn by a magnet. He paused at the chair. He ran his hand over the seat, then up the back. His fingers came away with only smears of dust.

Standing by the window, LaCrosse wiped at the dark film of accumulated dirt and looked out at the small, fenced backyard adjoining a half dozen others just like it.

Laundry hung from neighboring clothes lines. Dogs barked. Sunlight glinted off shards of broken bottles buried amid the weeds.

LaCrosse heard the slow drone of a plane passing overhead.

As he heard Buck come up behind him, Frank said, "He was a lot of things, but he wasn't a liar."

"He was a killer, Frank."

Frank was defeated and now he knew it. Olmstead was right.

The man was just a killer. There was no reason to believe he'd been leveling with him.

LaCrosse turned to go. He would have to accept reality now. He knew he had no choice.

At that moment he heard the sound of children's voices coming from another yard behind the house.

He paced back to the window and saw a woman open the back door of the house directly behind the one they were in. A gaggle of small children—some black, some white, one Latino—immediately darted down a short, rickety flight of wooden stairs into the yard.

Broken toys were strewn there, a rough playground for what looked liked the run-down neighborhood's best effort at a day-care center.

Unlocking the door, LaCrosse stepped into the back lot of the house. He shambled over to the picket fence separating the two yards.

Finding a plastic milk crate and upending it, LaCrosse climbed on top and looked over the fence.

LaCrosse watched the children play for a few moments, his spirits sinking.

None were his boy.

He was about to step down when his heart suddenly missed a beat.

Another child had just come toddling out from the back door of the house. He climbed bravely down the steps to play with the others.

A smiling, dark-haired boy about three years old. He was clutching a dirty patchwork baby quilt.

Tears began to well in LaCrosse's eyes. The hallway and the light. Like a tunnel. That was the other clue in Bob's photograph.

"Andy," he heard himself call out. "Andy!"

The boy looked up. Their eyes embraced each other.

It was his son.